"You're killing me..."

Jake's voice was as rough as sandpaper. He let his button-down shirt fall and then kicked his pants off and out of the way.

Rebecca's gaze moved down to his thigh even as she ran her fingers over her bare tummy. Jake tensed as he waited for her verdict.

"Are you going to just stand there staring?" she asked.

"I don't know what to do first," he said. "You're stunning."

For all that she was driving him wild, the hint of a blush that warmed her cheeks was almost more than he could bear. "That's a pretty good place to start..." she said as she covered the distance between them.

"But an even better place would be in the bedroom."

Dear Reader,

Welcome to the next story in the It's trading men! trilogy. We're in the second month of trading men on trading cards with the St. Marks Lunch Exchange group of single women in midtown Manhattan, and a new batch of hot hunks have just entered the dating pool!

I'm so excited to introduce you to Rebecca Thorpe and Jake Donnelly. Rebecca is the CEO of a large philanthropic foundation, and at twenty-eight, she's not willing to settle for anything less than the perfect man. So far, several have come close, but none have had that magic *something.*

When she sees Jake Donnelly on a trading card, she falls instantly in lust. He's completely wrong for her. Jake's a former NYPD detective, wounded in the line of duty, who lives in Brooklyn. He doesn't care about the social registry or where she got her degree. He's the man of Rebecca's most wicked dreams, and she can't wait to cut loose with Jake for one night of carnal indulgence. Only, they both soon realize that one night won't be nearly enough....

I hope you enjoy the fantasy and fun of *Have Me,* and continue on with *Want Me* in April.

As always, I can be reached at joleigh@joleigh.com. Hearing from readers is the best thing ever!

Love to you all,

Jo Leigh

Jo Leigh

HAVE ME

TORONTO NEW YORK LONDON
AMSTERDAM PARIS SYDNEY HAMBURG
STOCKHOLM ATHENS TOKYO MILAN MADRID
PRAGUE WARSAW BUDAPEST AUCKLAND

ISBN-13: 978-0-373-79675-5

HAVE ME

This edition published by arrangement with Harlequin Books S.A.

For questions and comments about the quality of this book please contact us at Customer_eCare@Harlequin.ca.

www.Harlequin.com

Printed in U.S.A.

ABOUT THE AUTHOR

Jo Leigh is from Los Angeles and always thought she'd end up living in Manhattan. So how did she end up in Utah, in a tiny town with a terrible internet connection, being bossed around by a houseful of rescued cats and dogs? What the heck, she says, predictability is boring. Jo has written more than forty novels for Harlequin Books. She can be contacted at joleigh@joleigh.com.

Books by Jo Leigh

HARLEQUIN BLAZE

2—GOING FOR IT
23—SCENT OF A WOMAN
34—SENSUAL SECRETS
72—A DASH OF TEMPTATION
88—TRUTH OR DARE
122—ARM CANDY
134—THE ONE WHO GOT AWAY
165—A LICK AND A PROMISE
178—HUSH
227—MINUTE BY MINUTE
265—CLOSER...
289—RELENTLESS
301—RELEASE
313—RECKONING
345—KIDNAPPED!
386—COMING SOON
398—HAVE MERCY
424—MS. MATCH
516—SEXY MS. TAKES
571—SHIVER
628—HOTSHOT
665—CHOOSE ME

To Yael.
I strive to create heroines who are as terrific as you.

1

Where R U???

REBECCA THORPE DIDN'T bother returning her friend Bree's text because there was no need. She was already walking up the pathway to the St. Marks church basement, the ready-to-be-frozen lunches she'd prepared in a large tote in preparation for the bimonthly lunch exchange. That wasn't what had slowed her pace though. She took her hand out of her coat pocket and stared again at the trading card she'd been toying with for the past fifteen minutes.

Ever since Shannon Fitzgerald had introduced the idea of using trading cards for trading *men,* the lunch exchange group, now numbering a whopping seventeen women, had been in a dating frenzy. The concept was simplicity itself: everyone involved recommended men they knew who were eligible and in the market. Whether they were relatives, friends or even guys without that perfect chemistry—for them at least—there was suddenly a bounty of prescreened, fully vetted local men. None of whom knew that they were members of this very select group.

On paper Gerard had seemed ideal. He was gorgeous, not only on the front of the card, either. Tall, dark, handsome, he'd gotten his degree from Cambridge, then had come to New York to work for the United Nations. He was urbane, sophisticated, dressed like a dream. And he'd taken her to dinner at Babbo, which was never a bad thing.

Sadly, like the other three men Rebecca had gone out with, courtesy of the trading cards, there had been no sizzle. Maybe she'd see Gerard again because he was fascinating, and they had many common interests, but the man she was looking for wasn't him. She'd known ten minutes into the date that the magic was missing, and while she'd been disappointed, she hadn't been surprised.

She was too picky. Or something. She couldn't spell out her criteria for *the one* but she certainly knew when she hadn't found it. She'd never had luck with men, and that had as much to do with her being a Winslow as it did with her taste, but the end result was that she hadn't truly connected with a man, not for the long haul, and the trading cards hadn't changed her luck.

So, with all due respect to the trading cards and to the whole idea of dating, she was done. No more cards for her, no more setups, no more blind dates, no more searching and no more hoping.

If she met someone in the course of doing what she loved, then great. If she didn't, she was fine with that, too. At twenty-eight she wasn't willing to say she'd never try again. She wanted to have a partner, maybe even have kids. But for now? Work was enough. Work was almost too much. It barely left time for her to visit with friends, go to movies, the theater, read a book. She was taking herself out of the game.

Determined and damn cold, she walked into St. Marks. The sound of women, of her friends, greeted her the moment she stepped over the threshold. There was a lot of joy to be had in her world, and only a part of it depended on a man.

"There you are," Bree said, grinning as she met Rebecca at one of the long tables. "Charlie bet me you wouldn't make it today. He said the donor dinner is getting too close."

Rebecca started stacking the lunches she'd prepared. "What did you win?"

"Something juicy that would make you blush."

Rebecca was glad not to have to hear the details. Charlie Winslow was her cousin, and while he was her favorite cousin, and she'd played an integral role in getting him and Bree together, there were certain things she'd rather not have in her memory. "As long as you're happy, I'm happy. And he's right. The dinner is driving me insane. I hate this part. I despise having to ask for money."

"Hard to run a charitable foundation without funds," Bree said.

"I know. But it defeats the purpose if I have to wine and dine the donors to the tune of several hundred thousand dollars. That money should be used elsewhere."

Bree, who looked adorable in skinny jeans with a gorgeous camel cowl-neck sweater, patted Rebecca's arm. "You could always serve them dinner á la soup kitchen. As a statement."

"I've considered it. But I really do need their money. Besides, the Four Seasons isn't known for its soup-kitchen ambience."

"Keep thinking about how much good the Winslow Foundation does. Then suck it up."

Rebecca laughed, as Shannon, the most important member of the lunch exchange, came plowing through the door. The redhead didn't know how to make anything but a dramatic entrance.

"I have new cards!" she said, lifting up a box from her family's printing shop. "Brand-new delicious men. You guys have outdone yourselves this time. Truly."

Rebecca pulled out Gerard's card, which had been in the second batch of trading cards. The first exchange had happened in February, a couple of weeks before Valentine's Day. As this was only the group's third exchange, it was too early to say how successful the new venture would be overall, but none of the dates had been disasters, and that was something.

She headed toward the front table where the cards were spread out for the taking, indecisive about putting Gerard back into the mix. For a moment, she was tempted. Tempted to forget she'd decided only minutes ago that she was done with all this. Maybe one more try? But that thought was dismissed the moment she remembered what she had waiting for her back at the office. Even if she wanted to try again, now wasn't the time. The dinner, which was more of a banquet complete with orchestra and dancing, was in just over a week, and if she found time to sleep between now and then, it would be a miracle.

Someone—Bree?—pushed into her from behind into the long table. "Hey, jeez." What was this, sale day at Barneys? Rebecca dropped Gerard's card on top of the pile and was in the process of getting out of the way when a tiny little tap stopped her.

She picked up the trading card resting against her hip. Then she stared. The name on the top was Jake Donnelly. The picture made all her female parts stand up and take notice. So to speak. Because he was the single most attractive man she'd ever seen. Ever. He wasn't the handsomest, but handsome was easy, handsome was proportions and ratios and cultural biases. No, Jake Donnelly was the man who fit *her*. She hadn't realized until right now that she'd carried a blueprint in her brain, made of exacting specifications down to the texture of his eyebrows.

They were on the thick side, dark. As dark as his hair, which was parted, long on the collar, unstudied, and, oh, who was she kidding, it was his eyes. They were an astonishing blue. Not pale, but a vibrant, piercing cerulean. The rest of his face was great, fabulous, a perfect frame; rugged enough that the parts of her that weren't transfixed by his eyes were doing a happy dancc about the rcst.

A happy dance? Okay, so it wasn't a sale at Barneys, it was high school and she was swooning over the quarterback. Even when she'd been in high school she hadn't swooned. This was unprecedented in every way.

She blinked. Took in a much-needed breath. Looked around. Just like in the movies, sounds returned, the picture in her hand wasn't the only thing in focus and she was Rebecca once more.

Almost.

She turned the card over, found out Donnelly had been recommended by Katy Groft. Rebecca made her way through the tightly packed crowd and sidled up to Katy, an NYU postgrad studying physics.

"Oh, you found Jake."

"Please tell me he looks like this picture."

Katy grinned. "Oh, he's even better."

"Oh, God." Rebecca didn't dare look to see which

category he fell in…marrying kind, dating or one-night stand. Not until she asked "Is he already taken?"

"Nope. You're in luck."

"Thank God. Because wow. He is…"

Katy sighed. "It pains me, it truly does. Because he's a sweetheart and he's funny, decent and very discreet. But he doesn't want a relationship at all. He's extremely private, too, so if that's going to bother you—"

"Private's good. Private and discreet is even better. Can you call him? Oh, he's probably at work now."

"Did you not read the back of the card?"

Rebecca felt a little blush steal across her cheeks. "Um…" She turned it over.

* His favorite restaurant: *Luigi's Pizza in Windsor Terrace.*
* Marry, date or one-night stand: *One night.*
* His secret passion: *No idea. But he's renovating his father's house in Brooklyn between jobs.*
* Watch out for: *Nothing, actually. He was great. I found him through my uncle whom I trust beyond measure.*
* Why it didn't work out: *Nothing scary here. Hot and fun. He's not sure what he's going to do with his life.*

Katy laughed, which made Rebecca tear her eyes away from Jake's picture.

"What?" she asked.

"Nothing," Katy said. "I'll call him right now."

"That would be very, very good."

THE SINK WASN'T COOPERATING. It was a heavy sonofabitch, and he couldn't just drop it into the new vanity, but the guy on the DIY DVD was talking too fast and Jake needed to rewind to get that last bit. He shifted the sink in his arms until it was balanced between him and the wall, unfortunately on his bad leg, then reached for his laptop. A second before his finger reached the touch pad, his walkie-talkie squawked. "Jake?"

Jake swore, which he'd been doing a lot this morning. This week. This month. It was his father. Again. About to tell him another idiotic cop joke.

Jake would have preferred not to hear another joke. Not while he was installing his old man's sink in the new master bath. In fact, not while he was still able to hear. But that's not how this gig worked.

He paused the DVD, lowered the sink to the floor and pressed the transmit button. "Okay, let's hear it."

There was a muffled giggle, a hell of a sound coming from a man who was sixty-three years old. "How many Jersey cops does it take to screw in a lightbulb?"

Jake sighed. This particular joke seemed to be stuck on repeat, as this was the third time he'd heard it in so many days. "How many?"

Now the laughter wasn't subdued and it wasn't only his old man laughing. The other two voices belonged to Pete Baskin and Liam O'Hara, all old farts, retired NYPD, bored out of their stinking minds and drunk on nothing but coffee and dominoes. "Just one—" his dad said.

"But he's never around when you need him," finished Liam.

The three of them laughed like asthmatic hyenas. The worst part about it? Someone had to be pushing the transmit button the whole damn time in order for Jake to hear it.

"Yo, Old Men?" he said, when he could finally get through.

"Who you calling old?" Pete yelled.

"You three. I'm trying to put in a sink. You know how much this sink weighs? I don't want to hear one more goddamn cop joke, you got it? No more. I swear to God."

"Yeah, yeah," Liam said. "Mikey always said you had no sense of humor."

"Well, I think he's damn funny looking, so I guess he's wrong about that, too."

"I can still whip your ass, Jacob Donnelly," his father said, "and don't you forget it."

Jake went back to the computer, replayed the section about the plumbing, then squared off against the sink. It hung off the wall, so the wheelchair wouldn't be an issue. In fact, the spigot was motion-controlled so his dad wouldn't have to touch anything if his hands were acting up.

Jake had already widened the door leading into the new master bath. It used to be a guest bathroom before his dad's rheumatoid arthritis started getting so bad. The wheelchair wasn't a hundred percent necessary yet, but soon his father wouldn't be able to make it up to his bedroom on the second floor, even with Jake's help.

He picked up the damn heavy sink and moved it over to the semipedestal, the plumbing all neatly tucked behind the white porcelain. It actually set easily, and since he'd been getting better with this plumbing business, he didn't find it necessary to curse the entire time he secured the top to the pedestal.

The problem wasn't the tools, but the pain. As soon as he could, he stood, stretching out the damaged thigh. The bullet had been a through and through, but what they don't say on TV is that it goes through muscle and tendon and veins and arteries on its quick voyage into, in his case, a factory wall. At least the thigh was less complicated than the shoulder wound.

Sometimes he felt as if it would have been better for everyone if the bastard had been a better shot. He rolled his left shoulder as his physiotherapist, Taye, taught him to do, then did a few stretches. This DIY crap had never been his bailiwick, but his dad needed the house to work for him, and the doctors had all thought it would be good for Jake to use his body to build something tangible.

Jake had realized when he was widening the wall that he actually liked remodeling. That was quite satisfying. The actual work itself though sucked like a Dyson.

But this was his life now. Crazy old men on the porch, fixing every problem the world had ever known. It didn't matter that it was March and as cold as hell outside; they kept on playing their bones, the space heater barely keeping them from hypothermia. Of course they had their cold-weather gear on. These men had been beat cops in so many New York winters the cold didn't stand a chance.

Thank Christ for electric blankets. 'Cause Mike Donnelly, for all his bluster, was getting on. It would be good when Jake had the new shower finished. Nothing to step over, nothing his crooked hands couldn't handle. Then he'd be able to jack up the heating bill to his heart's content, shower three times a day if he wanted.

In the meantime, there was plumbing to do. Jake limped over to the laptop and continued the how-to. Two minutes in, his cell rang. It was Katy Groft, which was weird. They'd gone out, it had been fine, but Jake had been pretty damn clear about his intentions. He wasn't one of those guys who said they'd call, then blew it off. None of that bullshit. "Hello?"

"Hey, Jake. Got a minute?"

"Sure."

"I'm sending you a picture."

"Okay." His phone beeped a second later. "Hold on." He clicked over to the photo, and what he saw surprised him even more than the phone call itself. It was... what's her name, the Winslow who wasn't called Winslow. Thorpe. That's right. Rebecca Thorpe. Ran some kind of big foundation or something, was always in the papers, especially the *Post.* What he didn't know was why Katy Groft would want him to see Thorpe's picture. "Okay," he said again.

"This is my friend Rebecca," Katy said. "Interested?"

"In what?"

"Her. Going out with her. You know, a date?"

He stared again at the phone, at the picture. Rebecca Thorpe was a beautiful woman. Interesting beautiful. Her face was too long, her nose too prominent, but there was something better than pretty about her. Every picture he'd seen of her, didn't matter who she was with, she seemed to be daring everyone to make something of it. Of her. Right now, looking at the overexposed camera phone photo, he had to smile. No choice. It didn't hurt that she had a body that struck all the right chords. Long, lean, like a Thoroughbred. "You do realize you called Jake Donnelly, right?"

Katy laughed. "Yes. I'm very aware of who you are. And who she is. And I happen to believe you two would hit it off well. I'm pretty clever about these things. And don't worry, she already understands you're not in the market for anything serious."

So this Thoroughbred wanted to go out with a quarter horse for a change of pace? "She knows I'm busted up, right?"

"Not a problem."

He gave it another minute's thought, then figured, "Sure. Why the hell not?"

"Great. How about the Upstairs bar at the Kimberly Hotel, tomorrow night at eight?"

It was his turn to laugh. "What is this, some kind of gag?"

"No. I swear. She's great. You'll like her. A lot."

He'd have to wear something nice to the Kimberly. But he hadn't worn anything nice in a long time. Before he got shot, that's for sure. "I'll get there a little early. Introduce myself."

"Excellent. You'll thank me."

"I'm already thanking you. For thinking of me. Although I'm still unclear why."

"You'll see," she said.

"Fair enough." He disconnected from Katy, but stared at the picture on his phone for a while. God damn, she was something else.

Katy had been only the second woman he'd been with since he'd been put out to pasture. She'd been great, and if his life had made any kind of sense, he might have pursued more than a onetime thing. But the only thing he knew for sure at the moment was that he was a broken ex-cop without a plan in the world except for rebuilding the house he was born in so his father could live out the rest of his days at home. After that was anybody's guess.

"Hey, Jake?"

He winced at the sound of his father's voice, tinny over the walkie. "Yeah, Dad," he said, his thumb finding the transmit button without his even having to look.

"How many cop jokes are there?"

He shoved his cell into his pocket. "Two," Jake said. "All the rest of them are true."

Laughter filled the mess of a bathroom, and Jake supposed that as far as problems went, having three lunatics telling him cop jokes all day was pretty far down the list.

2

REBECCA ARRIVED AT HER building just before 6:00 a.m. She needed coffee and lots of it. Facing her to-do list was not something she was looking forward to but there was no getting around it.

Her suite on 33rd was a behemoth. The size itself wasn't the issue—it was the fussy ostentation that got to her, the image that nearly outweighed their purpose. There was an enormous fresh-flower display next to the huge mahogany reception desk. Warren, the receptionist, wouldn't be in until eight-thirty, and Rebecca's personal assistant, Dani, had been coming in at eight lately, an hour earlier than she had to. It was very, very still with no one else on the floor, but then that wasn't unusual. The air of gravitas was nurtured like a living thing in this fortress.

Rebecca didn't make a sound on the plush burgundy carpeting in the long hallway that led to her office. She swiped her key card, put her briefcase on her desk, her purse in her credenza drawer, and went to the small private room—the truest symbol of how much the founders had prized their creature comforts. She headed straight for the coffeemaker.

Once she'd finished with the prep and pressed the button for the machine to start brewing, she turned and leaned on the counter. There was a huge LED television mounted on the wall across from the deep and supremely comfortable leather chairs, museum-worthy paintings on the muted walls and a couch with such deep bottom cushions that it was more suitable to napping than sitting. Fresh flowers were here as well, replaced weekly by a service that understood decorum while making a point that when it came to the details, no expense was spared. It was as ridiculous as it was sacrosanct.

She was the first woman to ever run the foundation, and her ideas about modeling their business plan after the great philanthropic organizations like the Rockefeller Trust or the Carnegie Group continued to be an uphill war. Picking her battles had been one of her first and most important lessons.

That's why she tried hard not to resent the time and money being spent on the donor dinner. The guest list included most of the *Forbes* top-fifty richest people in the world. They gave millions so that after all these years, their endowments were in the billions. She needed to remember that and just do the job.

Preparing her coffee in her favorite mug soothed her, letting her prioritize the next few unencumbered hours. It wasn't until she took her first sip that her thoughts turned to Jake. And there was a problem.

Not her excitement, that was a pleasure and a rush. It wasn't like her to want a man purely for sex. She was, in theory, at least to quote her mother, above that sort of thing.

Guess not, Mom.

When she returned to her desk, instead of clicking

on her email, she got her purse from the credenza and took out Jake's trading card.

Oh, yeah. She wasn't at all sure why, but looking at him made her clench all kinds of important muscles. She hadn't even met him and his face started a chemical spike inside her. The exact same reaction had occurred each time she'd sneaked a peek at his photograph. She refused to acknowledge how often that had been.

The problem was, with this level of excitement over the two-dimensional image, how on earth was the very three-dimensional living man going to measure up?

It was all about narrowing her expectations. She could do that. It wasn't as if she wanted to fall in love with Jake or for him to love her. She hoped to like him, though, because she knew from experience that if he was a complete jerk, her attraction would vanish in an instant.

They were going to meet for drinks and that was to her advantage. She didn't normally indulge to the point of feeling buzzed, but when she did, she became more forgiving. And, if it came down to it, she could probably get him to not talk at all.

She put his card away, determined not to look at it again until after work. Not only was she slammed for time, but she needed to get home early enough to go the extra mile with grooming. Oh, the joys and pains of getting naked with someone new.

She clicked on her email icon, and the sheer number of new messages was enough to chase away any thoughts of sweaty sex. Especially when the first of the emails was from her father. That never ended well.

THE MORNING COFFEE WAS already made by the time Jake limped his way down the stairs. It was freezing outside.

Sitting in the kitchen, his father was bundled up in a thick wool sweater and had a lap blanket tucked around his lower half as he warmed his hands on his old NYPD coffee mug.

"The weatherman says we're in for a cold one tonight."

Jake nodded as he fixed his mug. Two sugars, half and half. He didn't drink until he slid onto the banquette in the breakfast nook. He needed to do something about the cushion covers. They were almost as old as he was and the regular washings had made them threadbare and pale. "I'm going to the city."

"Yeah?" his dad asked.

"Yeah."

"Date?"

Jake drank some coffee, sighing in satisfaction as it warmed him. "Yeah."

"I'll get Liam to spend the night, then?"

"Already cleared it with him. He's bringing over DVDs."

"Ah, shit," his father said, putting his mug down on the counter, then turning his wheelchair a few degrees so he faced Jake. "That means another goddamn Bruce Willis festival. Swear to Christ, Liam has, a whatchamacallit, a bromance, going with that guy."

"What's it matter? Pete's got a hard-on for his car."

"Yeah." Mike picked up his cup again. "Everybody's got something. Except you. What do you got a hard-on for, Jake?"

"What the hell kind of a question is that?"

"Watch the tone. I'm still your father. I'm wondering, that's all. You spent a lot of time wanting to be in vice, then all those years doing undercover work. I'm thinking there's gotta be something else now. Something, please God, more interesting than Bruce Willis movies."

Jake drank some more coffee, not sure how to answer the question. If he should answer at all. But no, he would. He and his dad had spent a lot of years being distant. What with the work, then with Mom dying of cancer, and Jake having to be so hush-hush about everything. He'd decided to fix up the house by himself because he wanted to know his old man. Wanted someone to know him in return. Now was not the time to back off. "I don't know, Dad. I got nothing. Just the house."

"That's not gonna last forever."

"Nope. But it's something to do while I learn how to be a civilian."

"I hear that."

Jake nodded in tandem with his father. It wasn't easy, this talking thing. But dying alone in a warehouse filled with drug dealers wasn't easy, either. He could do this. The worst that would happen? He'd look like an idiot. He already did that without trying. "I've got a date tonight," he said. "She a looker."

"Good for you," Mike said. "Nice woman?"

"Never met her. Comes highly recommended, though."

"Yeah?"

"She's a Winslow."

"*Those* Winslows?" His dad settled his cup snugly on his lap as he wheeled over to the nook. "What the hell does one of those Winslows want with you?"

Jake laughed. "No idea. Looking forward to finding out."

"Probably heard who your old man was. Couldn't resist."

"You keep telling yourself that. See what happens."

Mike awkwardly put the cup on the table, and Jake

held back his wince. It was getting harder for his father to hold the damn mug at all, as his fingers twisted and bent. But there was no use crying about it. There wasn't a cure, and the medicines and physical therapy could do only so much. Retrofitting the house was what Jake could do, was doing.

"You know Sally Quayle? Three doors down, her husband was killed in Afghanistan last year?"

"Oh, no, Dad. Come on. We talked about this."

"We did, and we agreed."

"I'm not goddamn Santa and I'm not the neighborhood fixer. In case you haven't noticed, I'm also busy."

"There's always time to do right. She's worried about being alone. Thinking of buying a gun."

"Ah, crap. You want me to go talk to her."

"I do. We all do. She needs to know how dangerous that could be. Go over her house security. Make sure she's safe, yeah?"

Jake sighed. "Yeah, yeah. I'll go over this week. After I get a good start on the new shower." Why was it the only time Jake sounded like he was from Brooklyn was when he was home? He'd had the accent scared out of him at St. Francis Xavier high school, but it always came back the moment he was in the neighborhood.

"This week is fine. And don't start anything too big on the shower this afternoon. You need to look your best tonight."

"I what?"

Mike sniffed. "You're my only son. And a certified hero. She should know who she's dealing with, this Winslow woman."

What could Jake say? "Sure thing, Dad. I'll shave and everything."

REBECCA PAID THE CAB DRIVER, then got out on East 50th Street at the entrance to the Kimberly Hotel. She'd chosen it because the rooftop bar had spectacular views of Midtown. Also she liked the way they made their gimlets here with a very unique lime cordial. It didn't hurt that their luxury suites were gorgeous, the feather beds to die for. Even if magic didn't happen between her and Jake, she'd enjoy staying the night by herself, and if that happened, she already decided she'd be utterly decadent with room service.

With that in mind, she went inside, her gaze lingering on the lobby's beautiful grandfather clock as she went to the front desk. She handed them her overnight bag and her coat to put in her room. Registration took no time at all and once her key card was in her purse, she went to the lobby restroom. She had to remind herself that whatever happened would be fine, that if he was an ass, she'd lose nothing but a fantasy. Still, she wanted that fantasy, so she freshened her lipstick, fluffed her hair, checked her breath and let her heart pump and her hopes soar as she caught the next ride up.

It was the express to the roof, not giving her much time to think, which was good. There were only three men in business attire aboard, none of them speaking, although she had the feeling they'd been in the same meeting. They all looked as though they'd been to the battlefield and lost and that drinks at the penthouse bar would be a just reward.

Her nerves hit what she hoped was their peak as they reached the thirtieth floor. It was all she could do not to take Jake's trading card out of her purse and hold on to it like a talisman. Not that she wouldn't recognize him. She'd practically memorized his face. He'd look good on the roof with the blue and white fairy lights under the glass domed ceiling, with the city skyline behind him.

Frankly, he'd look good in a crumbling boiler room. But as long as she was making this into some kind of romantic one-night dream date, she might as well have the proper setting.

Another thing she liked about Upstairs at the Kimberly was that the music wasn't deafening. They catered to a more mature crowd and had some respect for eardrums. It was a bar made for getting to know a person.

The elevator opened at one minute past seven. There were several areas where Jake could be. On the main floor, at one of the tables, at the light-bedazzled bar itself or on one of the leather couches to either side of the bar. She ran her hands down her black sheath dress as she walked into the middle of the room. She glanced to her right, and there he was. He'd scored a hell of a table, one close to the window that looked out at the Chrysler building.

It was too dark to see the color of his eyes, but she could tell he looked pretty much as advertised. Dark scruffy hair, broad shoulders with a well-fitting jacket, a light button-down shirt tucked into dark trousers. He saw her and stood, and yep, he had slim hips and long legs. Even at this distance, he was hotter than hell, and *please, please, let this not crash and burn in the first five minutes.*

She hoped he would be equally impressed as she crossed over to him. He took a few steps himself, careful to keep close enough to the table to prevent poaching. It wasn't until the third step that she noticed his limp.

Katy hadn't said anything. Meaning she didn't deem it noteworthy. Rebecca had no problem with that. It was an interesting detail, something to discover by layers.

"Rebecca," he said, and goodness, yes, that was a great voice. Deep and mellow and she thought about one of her recent not-so-wonderful blind dates that hadn't been helped by Sam's unfortunately high and sadly nasal tone.

"Jake," she replied as she took his hand. It was warm and large, and the shake just firm enough. He also knew when to let go. Big plus. He almost touched the small of her back as he held her seat, giving her the best view.

He sat across from her. The candles on the table gave a hint of his eye color, but she'd need real lights for that. Later. Now was for talking. And drinking because her heart was pounding a bit too hard for her to ignore.

Before they had a chance to start the opening volley, a waitress came to the table. Rebecca ordered her vodka gimlet and Jake ordered a bourbon and water. Nice. Traditional. Masculine.

The second they were alone, he leaned a little toward her. "I'm never great with openings," he said. "I've always thought there should be rules, a standard pattern that all blind dates have to follow. Like school uniforms or meeting the queen. It would make things so much simpler."

She thought about her trading card, and how that had helped, and wondered if Jake knew he was on a card, if he'd approve. She thought, yes. "You're right. It's an excellent idea and should be implemented immediately. What say we start with the basics. The front page of the questionnaire. I'm Rebecca Thorpe, I live in Manhattan and work in the East Village. I'm an attorney although I don't practice, and I was born and raised here in the city. I've known Katy for over a year, and she's terrific, so I trusted her when she told me we might hit it off. I'm not looking for love, or for more than an interesting evening, which I hope is what you're after, and...well. That's about it."

His laughter suited her down to her toes. It was genuine, easy, relaxed. His smile was even more delicious than his picture had implied. So far, so good. But now, it was his turn.

"I'm Jake Donnelly, I'm currently living in Windsor Terrace in Brooklyn, in the house where I was born. I'm staying with my dad doing some remodeling work. I come from a long line of cops, all the way back to when the Donnellys crossed over from Ireland. I've been with the police department since I graduated college. Well, until earlier this year. I have no idea what I'm going to do after I finish the renovations."

He leaned back as their drinks were placed on the table, then sought her eyes again. "And it appears we're both looking for a night to remember. How'd I do?"

"Great," she said, then she lifted her glass and clicked it against his. Jake was totally unlike anyone she'd ever dated. He was from Brooklyn, but he'd given up the accent for something far easier on her admittedly snobbish ears. She knew absolutely nothing about being a cop, about Windsor Terrace, about renovations. She was incredibly curious to know if his limp and no longer being a policeman were connected. And she couldn't imagine, not for the life of her, staying with her own family for more than about three hours. She and Jake were worlds apart, completely unsuited in every way but one.

He was *perfect.*

JAKE DRANK A LITTLE AS HE tried not to look as if he was scoping her out from head to toe. But screw it, he was. At least, as much as he could, given she was sitting.

Rebecca Thorpe was, to put it bluntly, off the charts hot. Her hair was golden and shiny in the glitter of the bar, her eyes smoky and intense. She was tall and slender, but the way her dress hugged her breasts made him say a prayer this night would end with him learning a lot more.

No mention of the Winslow name or the foundation she headed. Why not? Being careful? Probably, although why she would assume he didn't recognize her was a little baffling. Everyone who lived in New York knew of her family. They were like the Kennedys. Politicians, judges, private jets, private clubs, more money than sense if you asked him, but nobody did, and that seemed fair. He wouldn't know what the hell to do in a room full of Winslows, but being right here, right now with this one? It was his lucky day.

"I don't know where to start with questions," Rebecca said. "Do you miss being a cop?"

He'd left himself open for whatever with that intro, but he still wished she'd begun somewhere else. He shouldn't complain. At least she hadn't opened with the limp.

He was still self-conscious about the scars. Odd how the shoulder looked so much worse. The leg was no picnic, either. But it hadn't made anyone run screaming. Yet. What the hell, if it freaked her out, there was nothing he could do about that. He'd just get on home and read up on shower installations. "Yeah, I miss it," he said. "Hard not to, when it's the only thing I've ever done. I could have taken a desk assignment, but that wasn't me."

"Ah, so you were hurt on the job?"

He nodded. "Yeah. Shot in the thigh and the shoulder. They're not pretty, but I was lucky. Either one could have killed me, so…"

"I can't imagine. God, shot twice?" She shuddered, winced. "That's horrible. I'm always astonished at how vulnerable the human body can be, while at the same time astoundingly strong. I had a friend once who slipped on a leaf. Fell. Hit her head. She was twenty-four, and she died that night. You were shot twice, and you not only survived, but it looks from here as if you're thriving."

"It is a mystery. I tell people it must not have been my time, but that's just something easy to say. I'm not a religious man, or one who believes in fate. Nothing mystical or predestined. I guess I'm a pragmatist. I was in a dangerous profession, in a risky situation. It's no big surprise I was wounded. I lived because they got to me in time, got me to the right doctors. Thriving? Well, I wouldn't go that far, but I'm learning to accept my limitations. Oddly, there are fewer than I expected, with the notable exception of losing my career."

She didn't respond immediately, but she did lean in. She didn't even try to pretend she wasn't staring, wasn't taking his measure. "A pragmatist," she said eventually. "That's helpful, living in this city. This world."

"It is. What about you?" he asked. "What do you believe in?"

She smiled, leaned back in her chair. Her bangs were a bit in her eyes and he wanted to push them back to see her better. Not complaining, just sorta wishing.

"Boy, you don't fool around, do you?"

"Guess not. We can always talk about this damn cold front, if you'd prefer."

"I'm good," she said. "I like the tough questions."

"I didn't even ask, would you like something to eat? I

haven't looked at the menu, but I know they serve food here. Or we could go somewhere else for dinner."

"Oh, food. I'm not starving, but I could eat something. How about you?"

"I could do with more than the bologna sandwich I had around four. Busy day."

"I happen to know the menu here is excellent. Why don't you see if anything suits your fancy. Meanwhile I'll consider my answer to your very provocative question and finish my drink."

He nodded, grabbed the menu from the center of the table. Not much he didn't like. When he looked up again, she was still staring at him. He should have been unsettled. He wasn't used to undisguised interest. In fact, his life had depended on his blending in, fading into the background. Even the dark wasn't enough to hide behind, but instead of getting that crawling itch to run, he wanted her to look her fill. And he wanted her to like what she saw.

He passed her the menu, then finished his bourbon, signaling the waitress when he caught her eye. "There's nothing on there I wouldn't eat," he said to Rebecca. "Could live without the foie gras, but I like the meat and the fish selections. I think you should pick us out a few, and we'll have ourselves a small buffet while we go at least one step beyond the surface. How does that sound?"

"Fantastic."

Their order was taken, fresh drinks requested, and they were alone once more. It was all he could do not to call back the lovely girl and ask her to add a room with a king-size bed to the tab.

"I'm a mutt," Rebecca said, folding her hands on the shiny table. "Philosophically. I lean toward Buddhism, but I've got some roots in the church from when I was a kid. I mostly try to make a difference. Walk the walk, not just talk about it. I tend to connect to people who do the same."

That could have been a crock of bull, but his instincts said no. She was telling him the truth. It fit with her job, but that wasn't what he thought she was talking about. Another skill from his vice days was how to listen for the truth. Of course, in this instance, he had to factor in how badly he wanted to take Rebecca Thorpe to bed.

Which was really damn bad.

3

REBECCA LICKED THE TIP OF her thumb as she finished the last of her salt cod fritter. She'd decided to play hardball with the ordering—all of it finger food. Zucchini fritters, lollipop lamb chops, decadent French fries, even the crisp baby artichokes. She'd picked up a lollipop first thing, watching him watch her bring the food to her mouth, take a bite. Gauntlet thrown, she sipped her second drink and waited to see what he'd do.

He started with a couple of fries. Slow moving, deliberate, and his gaze on hers never wavered. As he chewed, his jaw muscle flexed in a way that made her blush. He couldn't tell, not in this light, yet his thick right eyebrow rose along with the corners of his mouth.

She grinned back, pleased he'd decided to play. Somehow the music had become smoky jazz, and the heat from the temperature-controlled floor slipped up her dress all the way to her very pretty, very naughty La Perla panties.

Through it all, the ordering, the waiting, the cute young waitress flirting with Jake as she set down their plates, Jake hadn't once lost the thread of their conversation. Rebecca wasn't sure if they were at the third or fourth level now that they'd reached ex-lovers territory.

"She was great," he said, using his napkin. "And I like to think I'm a reasonably adventurous guy, but when she started talking plushies..." He shook his head, grabbed a tiny artichoke.

"Plushies. You mean dressing up like stuffed animals plushies?"

"I do. I hope that's not your thing, but I'd have to say right up front that nope, not gonna go there. I like my partners to be human. It's a radical stance, but one I'm not going to budge on."

"Where do you stand on aliens who look humanoid?"

He thought a minute. "Depends. Do they really look like humans, or are they lizard people in disguise?"

"I see your point. I always draw the line at shape-shifters. I include vampires in that, by the way."

"Damn. There goes my plans for the rest of the night."

She laughed again, charmed. Not so much at the obvious quip but at his delivery. Very dry. Very...sexy. "Nothing wrong with a little nip here and there," she said.

He cleared his throat and shifted in his chair. "I agree," he said, putting his napkin on the table. "Now, if you'll excuse me."

As he walked away, Rebecca let herself linger on the breadth of his shoulders, the length of his legs. He might have a limp, but there was still a swagger to him that had her crossing her legs.

When he got back, she would bring up the room. They hadn't eaten too much and had only two drinks each. If they wanted dessert later they could order from room service. Everything about the evening led her to believe he was amenable, even though they hadn't yet touched.

While she could, she retrieved her mirror from her purse. After a fresh coat of lipstick, she stuck a breath strip in her mouth, realizing too late that it didn't go with vodka gimlets. At all. A quick shudder, then she closed her purse, aware of the room itself for the first time since she'd stepped off the elevator.

There was a sizable crowd for a Tuesday night. Most everyone was in business attire, upscale. While she saw people on the prowl, the atmosphere was not that of a pickup bar. Here, the desperation wouldn't start until around 3:00 a.m.

She wondered what Charlie and Bree were doing and almost got out her cell to text, but no, Bree could wait on Rebecca's report. Tonight felt private, different. In other circumstances, she'd have felt this evening was a beginning. She liked him a lot. More than anyone she'd been out with in years.

On the other hand, maybe knowing this was a singular event had made this ease possible. They weren't at a relationship audition. Sex, yes, but she figured they'd nailed that about five minutes in.

The conversation had gone from philosophy to her explaining the intricacies of preparing lunches and trading them at a church basement, and then somehow they'd landed at exes. Hers, she realized, had all fizzled due to boredom. No, that wasn't fair. There had been reasons she'd gone out with those few men for longer than a handful of months, but there had been no grand passions. Weirdly, she'd felt perfectly comfortable telling Jake just that.

There he was. Smiling from across the room. She watched as he maneuvered through people and tables.

When he sat down, he covered her hand with his. "I took the liberty of booking a room here tonight. I won't lie and say I wouldn't be disappointed if you don't want to join me, but I'll also take it like a man."

She turned her hand over and squeezed his fingers. "The only problem with that is I already have a room here. And since I'm the one who instigated this evening, I win the coin toss."

He studied her for a long minute. "Wow. That's… Full disclosure, though. I lied about taking it like a man."

She grinned. God, he was adorable. "If you're finished, why don't I put this on the tab, and we go down to cancel your reservation?"

He fetched his wallet from his pocket. "I'll be taking care of this. But thanks for the offer."

They wrapped it up, he put on a dark knee-length coat she hadn't even noticed, then held the back of her chair while she stood. An old-fashioned move, but one she didn't mind. Especially because she was a little wobbly. Not from the booze; she hadn't had enough to faze her. From the touching. The "any second now, don't know where things are going to go" touching.

After she picked up her purse, he slipped his hand around hers. It wasn't like the handshake, not at all. It was just…wonderful.

WALKING WITH REBECCA TO the front desk reminded him of his prom. Not the dance, but afterward, going into the hotel in Brooklyn with Antoinette Fallucci on his arm. He'd been in a terrible borrowed tux that was too tight in the crotch even discounting the fact that he'd been seventeen, but Antoinette had looked like a princess in her strapless dress, and she'd been the homecoming queen, a cheerleader and without doubt the most beautiful and popular girl in his senior class. He'd strutted into that hotel. This time, he played it a little cooler, but he did feel that thrill, knowing he was with the best one, that every man in the place was jealous.

It had nothing to do with her being a Winslow. The subject hadn't come up and he didn't expect it to. Not when there were so many other interesting things to talk about.

He smiled as they waited for a desk clerk. She smiled in return and he wanted to kiss her. He'd stood close to her in the elevator, gotten a whiff of her perfume, and the effect still sizzled through his veins. He had no idea what the scent was, only that it made him want to spend a hell of a long time exploring that long, graceful neck of hers.

That they'd barely touched was both horrible and hot. He knew she'd be soft, but that was far too vague. How different soft was between the shell of an ear, the skin just under a belly button. His gaze drifted down as he realized there was no word for how it would feel to run his fingers across her inner thigh.

Shit, if he was going to be thinking like that, he should button his coat. Hide the evidence. Thankfully, the woman who'd made his reservation earlier called them to the desk.

"Is something wrong?" she asked.

"We double-booked. Miscommunication. I hope it's not too late to cancel."

"Mr. Donnelly, right?"

Surprised that she remembered his name, he nodded.

"I'll cancel that right now, sir. It'll be a moment."

Jake glanced at Rebecca. He liked that she was tall, five-eight, he'd guess? A six-inch difference was very doable. Not that anything couldn't be worked around.

He signed his name on the line, gave back the key card, and finally, they were free to leave.

"Thank you, Mr. Donnelly,"

"Yeah, thanks," he said, tearing his gaze from Rebecca, but he barely gave the other woman a second because his date, this amazing woman in the sleek black dress, tossed her hair behind her shoulder and tugged him along and it was as if the flag had been lowered in a race he hadn't known he was running. It took him two steps to catch up, and when they looked at each other, side by side, gripping each other's hands, they grinned like idiots. Who were going to have sex. Really, really soon.

"Should we order drinks?" she asked as they walked, their speed increasing with each step. "Champagne? Wine? Soda?"

"Wine? Do you like red? Although white would probably be better after vodka. Maybe we should just get some vodka."

"I like red." She pushed the elevator button three times, leaning into her thumb every time. "Besides, you're a bourbon man. Bourbon men don't drink vodka."

"Who told you such obvious lies? Whoever it was should be banished from ever tasting another shot of Stoli. And he shouldn't be able to look at a bottle of Elit."

The elevator dinged and opened. Finally. A couple walked out, ignoring them completely. It was Jake's turn to pull Rebecca inside.

"Then why did you order bourbon?" she asked.

He shrugged, astonished they were speaking in sentences when his brain and his body were one hundred percent focused on getting inside the goddamn room. "I like it."

"Okay." She pushed the button for the fifteenth floor. "What booze don't you like?"

He couldn't stand it, he pulled her until she was flush against him and he was staring down into her dark, wide eyes. "Boone's Farm."

She laughed as she pressed her breasts to his chest. He inhaled sharply at the feel of her, the reality of her. Then her hand, her right hand, slipped under his arm, around his waist and up his back. Without his permission, his hips jerked forward, his quickly hardening cock meeting the perfect resistance of her hip. Each floor they ascended felt like foreplay.

"What about you?" he asked, straining to pick up the thread of their conversation, although he was pretty sure if he started talking about pork belly futures neither of them would care. "Is there anything respectable you don't like?"

"Tons of things. But I suppose you're talking about liquor." Her breath whispered against his jaw, and that hand on his back was moving in small circles, the hint of friction electric. "Oddly," she said, her voice maybe half an octave lower than it had been a minute ago, "single malt Scotch whiskey. I know, it's very girlie of me, but I hate it. What's worse, I get very cranky when people get in my face about how superior it is. The age and what kind of barrel it was kept in. Which is ridiculous because I do the exact same thing with wine and champagne, so who the hell do I think I am? But there you have it. Completely irrational."

"Good to know," he said, now a few millimeters away from brushing his lips against hers. "I was going to seduce you with my knowledge of Glenlivet, but I won't now. Pity. I know a lot about Glenlivet, and I'm incredibly charming when I add the personal anecdotes."

"That's okay," she said, as they came to a smooth halt. "I already find you incredibly charming."

He'd have kissed her right then, right as they stepped out of the elevator, but he wanted it private. Not that anyone was in the hall. It didn't matter. He wasn't going to do anything to this woman until he had her alone and there was a bed nearby. He checked the wall plaque and followed the arrows to room 1562, at the very end of the hall. They didn't run, but they moved as quickly as his leg allowed.

She got the green light with her key card on the second try and he shoved the door open. His first impression of the room was that it was big for a Manhattan hotel and that it was very full with a sofa and chairs and coffee table, but it could have been the size of a pencil box and bright chartreuse and he wouldn't have cared. It was theirs, and while there wasn't a bed in front of him, there had to be one close. Rebecca walked in, but she didn't get far.

As he slammed the door shut behind him, he gave her a spin, a sweet little twirl that set her back against the door with him blocking her path.

Her smile said she didn't mind, and her lips parting as she raked his face with her very large eyes told him they were on the same page. She huffed softly as he slipped his hand behind her nape and his tongue in her mouth.

It was hot slick tongues and broken moans as they tried to get his coat off, both of them reaching at the same time. She scratched his wrist then shoved the coat off his shoulder while he was trying to remove the other side of the damn thing, and he twisted his shoulder in all the wrong ways.

He hissed as he drew back, hating his body so fucking much because he could be kissing her right now instead of this.

"I hurt you."

"You didn't. We did. I just have to be careful." He threw his coat with force onto one of the big chairs, then took off his jacket, as well. He turned his head as he reached for his shirt buttons, but her fingers on top of his made him look.

"We can be careful."

"It's the scars. Left shoulder, right thigh. I can keep my T-shirt on, turn off the lights—"

She slipped the top button through the hole. "Don't worry about my delicate sensibilities. I'm fine. As long as we can hurry up and get back to where we're getting naked together."

Scooping her into his arms, trapping her hands, he kissed her. Not that panic sloppy kissing, which was good, damn fine, but this was something else. This was a preview, a warning. He liked this part, and he was good at it. So he'd take it slow for the next few minutes, because soon, the moment he had that dress off her in fact, it was going to get crazy again. Messy, wet and hot, and while he couldn't do everything he used to, he could do plenty.

Her moan was low as she tussled with his tongue. He moved his hands under her hair until he found the top of her dress, the zipper hidden inconveniently behind a fold of material, but he was using his dominant hand, not the one with the intermittent quaver, so no problem. His cock hardened as the zipper lowered until it hit bottom. The feel of her skin beneath his palms made him groan, but when she pushed her hips against his aching erection, he decided the lesson was over, and all bets were off.

He pulled back, not letting her have another chance with his shirt.

"Fine," she said, chuckling, "be that way." Then she took two steps away and lifted her dress over her head and let it flutter to the floor.

Jake choked. It took him a minute of coughing to get his act together, and when he did, and he looked at her again, he had to consciously remember how to breathe. "Holy God."

"So you're a La Perla fan?"

"I have no idea what a La Perla is, but I'm over the moon about your underwear."

Her grin let him know she'd planned to knock him off his feet with the stunning bra and panties. Jesus, she was still wearing her heels, and the combination was enough to make a weaker man come without a touch.

The garments were sheerest white. Barely there, except for a small triangle that covered her pussy so he couldn't tell what she was hiding. He didn't give a damn. She could be hairy, bald as a cue ball or anything in between, it all worked as far as he was concerned. That he didn't know even with all that flesh on display made him insane.

The opposite was true on top. There was nothing but that sheer, sheer white covering her stunning breasts. Hard little nipples in the center of pink areolas like iced cupcakes with cherries on top.

And while staring at her was a wet dream all its own, there was so much more to be done. He tugged his shirt out from his trousers, toed off his shoes, then his socks, and by the time he'd unbuttoned the shirt with his right hand, his left had undone his belt and was working on his zipper.

Rebecca was most definitely not helping. In fact, she

was making it ridiculously harder to do this circus trick because whether she realized it or not, every move she made turned up the heat a notch. The sway of her hips as she took a single step, the roll of her shoulder, the shake of her head so her hair fluffed around her face. There wasn't a thing about her that didn't make him want to beg.

"You're killing me," he said, his voice as rough as sandpaper. He let his button-down fall, leaving him in his undershirt, and then his pants dropped and he kicked those out of the way.

Her gaze moved down to his thigh even as she ran her fingers over her bare tummy. Jake tensed as he waited for her verdict. She winced, but her hand didn't stop moving. He relaxed. She wasn't freaked out. His first date after had been, and he could never bring himself to blame her, but his gratitude that this woman hadn't run for the hills knew no bounds.

"Are you going to just stand there staring?" she asked.

"I don't know what to do first," he said. "You're stunning."

For all that she was driving him wild, the hint of a blush that warmed her cheeks was almost more than he could bear. "That's a pretty good place to start," she said as she covered the distance between them. "But an even better place would be in the actual bedroom."

He swung his arm around her neck and pulled her into a punishing kiss. His free hand went to the low line of her panties, the covered spot, and he slipped his fingers inside the material.

Ah. Not a full Brazilian then, but a landing strip. They needed to get to the bed before he came standing in his boxer briefs.

4

JAKE KISSED HER AS IF HE'D read her diary. All the things she hadn't written down. How that exact pressure made her shiver. How one of her favorite things was when it wasn't only thrusting, but teasing and nipping and licking and just plain wanting to feel *everything.*

His fingers brushing the small trail of hair made her quiver, and God, they needed to stop screwing around. She stepped back from the glorious kiss and took his hand out of her panties. "Now?" she asked. "Please?"

He laughed, dipped somewhat inelegantly to grab his slacks then pushed her along with his hand conveniently placed on her ass.

Finally, there was the king-size feather bed. It wasn't merely a gorgeous thing to sleep on. The plush headboard, which was actually a built-in feature of the wall, made for comfy bracing, if it should be needed. She hoped it would be needed.

"What are you grinning about?" he asked as he spun her around to face him.

"Happy. Excited. Wishing you were very much more naked than you are."

"I can do that," he said. "Here goes—if it's too much

a turnoff—well, I won't need therapy over it." He yanked his V-neck undershirt up his chest, quick, like taking off a bandage.

Rebecca was caught by the view of his slim waist, the lines of his abdominal muscles, the almost-but-not-quite-perfect four pack and the fact that he had actual hair on his chest. She swallowed at the blatant masculinity.

She, in turn, felt, well, gooey. Feminine. Small, hungry, attracted, girlie. She moved closer to him, unable to stop her fingers from touching his dark, slender line of hair that rose from just below his ribs until it spread to lightly cover his chest.

He gasped at the brush of her hand, and she watched his muscles shudder. Then he pulled the shirt off the rest of the way, revealing the scar at the top of his left shoulder. "The bullet barely missed the subclavian artery," he said. "Came in smooth, came out rough, but I was lucky. The doctor says eventually I should regain almost all my mobility."

She appreciated the heads-up. The small wound was puckered, red, shiny, but nothing horrific. Whereas his back, when he turned, wasn't nearly as neat. She exhaled hard, not from disgust but from sympathy. His skin was mottled; that same shiny red here though making it look more like a fresh burn than what it was. She raised her hand again, but paused an inch from his poor flesh.

Her gaze moved down to his thigh. That was a deep gouge, something ripped away, not like the torn and battered scarring on his shoulder. "Will it hurt?"

"To touch? No. It's mostly numb. Not a hundred percent, and sometimes something will press the wrong nerve. But you don't need to worry. That is, if you still want to—"

She leaned in then, letting her fingers brush the

strange terrain as she pressed her lips to the edge of his wound. "I'm sorry you were hurt."

"Me, too." He turned around slowly. "Onward?"

She was the one to cup his face, to ravish him with tongue and teeth and urgency.

"Well, damn." He kissed her again, once, hard, then stepped away, carefully maneuvering the waistband of his briefs over his straining cock. She couldn't look anywhere else but at his darkly flushed erection. There was moisture at the tip, his foreskin barely visible. "I'm going to start begging in a minute," he whispered.

She forced her gaze up. "We wouldn't want that."

He groaned low and loud, his cock jerking against his taut stomach. His hands went to her shoulders, gripping her firmly as he walked her to the bed. He paused before the back of her legs touched the mattress. "Okay, I can't… I love the…" He indicated her outfit with a sweeping glance up, down and up again. "That bra… Amazing. You're amazing. But it's got to go, because there isn't a thing I don't want to see. All right?"

She nodded, not able to do much more because he still held her arms.

Releasing her, he reached around and undid the bra's clasp. Then he kissed the curve of her neck with warm lips as he slipped the straps off her shoulders. The bra fell between them, floated down, touching her skin, and his, too, if his sharp hiss was anything to go by.

His gaze on her breasts, he huffed a breath before he swallowed. "Jesus. Rebecca."

She blushed again. The heat filled her cheeks and where was all her bravado and determination to be in charge of the night? She felt…shy? A little bit. Pleased, definitely. Not that she didn't want his praise, but in a moment she was going to duck her chin and twirl her hair because in all her fantasies of how things would go, she hadn't considered that she'd see him as so much more than the man on the card. She liked him, and even though there wasn't going to be a second date, she wanted him to like her in return. Not only the sex, but *her.*

She sent her panties to rest on top of her bra. The only thing he couldn't see now were her feet but that would change in a minute. He grinned, like he had in the hallway, and fell into a cloud of white down, bringing her along for the ride.

They kissed, deeper now, possessive and exploring and hungry. He sucked the very tip of her tongue, showing her how good he was with small things.

There were hands at play as well, hers brushing over his arms, his sides, down to the tapered waist and slim hips. She loved hip bones with their curves and shapes, but more than that she loved the unlimited access. She suspected he'd let her do anything, feel him anywhere. She could paint his toenails blue and he'd stay hard to the last little piggy. And if he wanted to return the favor? She'd probably quiver so much she'd have nail polish up to her ankles.

She laughed while he was teasing her lips, and he pulled slightly away. "What?"

"I'm already having the best time ever. You're…" She sighed. "You're fantastic."

The sound he made wasn't a word, but when he turned them both so she fell back on the feather bed, she gathered he liked the compliment.

"Condoms," he said. "Pocket." Then he rolled off the bed to his feet, and she got a show of his extraordinary butt as he rifled his trouser pockets.

"My," she said, when he turned around. His cock

looked exceptionally eager. It was well proportioned, longer and thicker than average, and it was straining so that with every move it tapped his belly, leaving a trail of liquid excitement behind.

She rose to her knees, unable to lay back passively when she was as eager as he was to discover the next sensation, to taste and to touch and to let herself be carried away.

He got back on the bed, ripping open the condom as he shuffled to the center, then he brought his lips so close to her ear she shivered with the warmth of his breath. "I want you to ride me. The first time. So I won't miss a thing."

Rebecca nodded. She'd thought it might be easier for him with his injuries, but that wasn't her main consideration at the moment. She wanted to watch him, as well. See the expression on his face as he entered her. "You need to put that on," she said, touching the rubber.

Jake slung another pillow where his head was likely to land, then eased the condom on his cock, hissing the whole time. As he straightened his legs, he put his hand on the base of his prick, holding it steady, and he eased back, his head canted so he would have a perfect view.

Rebecca wasn't particularly showy in bed, always a little too self-conscious, but something about Jake... Still on her parted knees, she took hold of her right nipple with her fingers. Two fingers. Her nips were hard enough that when she squeezed them, the tip poked out, swollen and dark pink.

"God damn," he said, his voice an endearing combination of breathless and raspy.

Her free hand moved slowly down her chest to her

tummy. She circled her belly button, then walked two fingers down and down until they reached her landing strip. She hadn't stopped with the nipple play, so Jake's gaze was going up and down, his lips parted as his breathing became more ragged.

He couldn't seem to help moving the hand on his cock. He stroked himself and it must have felt dangerous because the muscles in his jaw tightened and so did the tendons in his neck. Then he closed his eyes, groaning as if she were killing him dead. "Rebecca. I'm already going to embarrass myself with how fast I'm going to come. Do you really want that to happen before I'm inside you?"

She removed her hands from her body and she felt flushed with more than anticipation. She liked driving him crazy. Which was only fair. She was feeling kind of nuts herself.

"Point taken," she said. She crawled close to his body so she could kiss him one more time. It started slow and sensual, but it turned into hot and burning in seconds. "Ready?" she asked, her voice a breathy whisper.

"Dying."

She got into position, took over for his steadying hand by reaching behind and lowered herself so slowly her thighs trembled. Watching him every second.

His pupils were huge, his nostrils flared, his lips were parted and he sounded as if he'd just finished a marathon. It was fantastic.

She didn't want to look away from his face, but movement down below forced the issue. It was his muscles. Pectorals, abdominals. Clenching, trembling. Chest rising and falling like a piston, and there was a sheen of sweat that made her feel like the Vixen Queen of Planet Earth.

As much fun as it had been to watch him unravel, now all her attention had switched to her own body. Because, whoa. He wasn't lying there anymore, he was thrusting. Up. His hands had somehow gripped her hips when she wasn't looking, and he was moving her to suit himself. She didn't mind. At all.

"God, you're gorgeous," he whispered, and that was the voice she'd remember. The wobbly, wrecked croak that was just this side of recognizable speech. "Hot and wet and, Christ, when you grip me like that. Dammit… warn me next time. No, don't warn me. Do anything you want. Just make sure I haven't passed out. I don't want to miss any…ahhh."

That made her tighten like a vise and she leaned forward enough to where his cock rubbed her perfectly. She'd been so close that all it took was a slight thrust with her hips and she was coming, her head thrown back, her mouth open and gasping, keening in a pitch she didn't recognize.

When she could see again, she realized he'd come, too, and she'd wanted to watch. Dammit.

She fell sideways, sprawling, gasping away. She managed to turn her head to find him looking at her. Grinning like a very satisfied kid at Christmas. "That was…"

He nodded.

"Again?"

His eyebrows rose and he blinked at her. "I'm thirty-four, not seventeen."

"How long?"

He breathed for a while. Then grinned. "Give me half an hour. I'm feeling inspired."

"I'll order drinks."

"See if they have Red Bull."

She laughed. "I'm sure they can oblige."

Well, how was it?????

OMG, Bree! Lunch? Here? 1:30?

Ur making me wait? I HATE u!

U do not. Bring caffine & IV.

LOL. C U later.

REBECCA CLICKED OFF HER phone as she stared at her open briefcase. It felt as if she was forgetting something, but given the lack of any sensible amount of sleep, she had no chance of remembering. She shut the damn thing, aware of how much work she'd skipped in order to indulge her libido last night, then put on her coat. She'd meant to have been at the office for hours by now.

It had been worth it, though. She grabbed her purse and briefcase. There was no one in the elevator, but that would change as she headed down. It was eight-thirty already; she wanted the espresso she hadn't had time or patience to make for herself. The elevator stopped two floors down from her twenty-eighth-floor condo, and she exchanged the traditional noncommittal, no-need-to-speak smile with the man who was exceedingly proud of his Swiss watch. She had at one time known the brand, but all she could remember now was that it cost over a million bucks, and that this guy with his salt-and-pepper hair and his cashmere coat took every opportunity to flash his prize possession. It reminded her of a girl with a new engagement ring.

The elevator stopped at almost every floor, and everyone got very chummy by the time they reached the lobby. She was, of course, stuck in the back, and Mr. Swiss Watch's back was squishing her boobs. Thank goodness for the layers of coat and clothes between them because she only wanted to think about her boobs in terms of last night and Jake.

She smiled as she crossed the lobby, nodding at the concierge and the doorman before hitting the street. It was freezing even though there was no snow left on Madison Avenue.

What she should have done was immediately get in line for a cab, but what she did was cross the street, swimming with the tide of dark coats and clicking heels, to Starbucks. Inevitably there was a long line, but she was desperate.

While she waited, she took out her cell phone and called Dani, her assistant, who would be wondering where the hell Rebecca was. Dani would have called her by nine, but not before.

"You okay?" Dani asked immediately.

"Headache. Late night. Everything okay there?"

"Except for your to-do list, everything's great. Mr. Turner called, of course."

Rebecca sighed. Turner was in charge of catering at the Four Seasons. "What now?"

"Something to do with the gift baskets for the guests, but he wouldn't tell me what because I'm either a spy for another hotel or an idiot, I'm not quite sure."

"I'll call him when I get in. Do me a favor?"

"I'll start the coffee in fifteen minutes. Are you getting something to eat?"

"Yes, thanks."

"See you soon."

Rebecca tried not to yawn, which made her yawn, and then she decided, the hell with it, she was going to think about Jake. To say he'd left an impression was… well, leaving him at the crack of dawn had been ridiculously difficult.

They'd been outside, on a very public street, and still she hadn't been able to stop kissing him. She'd blamed him, of course, said it was all his fault, but it hadn't been. She'd gotten all tingly the moment her lips met his. Tingly. God, who even said that. No one, that's who.

The one very good thing he'd done was not ask for her phone number. Because that would have been stepping over the line. Last night was a one-night deal. Okay, so they'd technically had sex this morning in the shower, but that went under the rubric of one-night stand, so there was no need to get picky about it. The essence of the agreement, from both sides, had been that it was to be a singular event. Nothing more. One incredible, fantastic, amazing, toe-curling night. The end. Anything else was out of the question.

It would have been different if she was the kind of woman who regularly practiced recreational sex. She knew a lot who did, but she wasn't one of them. First of all, she had too much on her plate as it was, and second, it never worked, not really. *Sex and the City* tried to glorify it, but in the end, all that fooling around didn't amount to much.

She'd rather do without, thanks.

But goodness, if there was ever a man who appealed in a *Sex and the City* way, it was Jake. She closed her eyes as she pictured the way he'd looked at her with so much hunger she'd forgotten how to breathe. His hands on her bottom in the shower, such big hands, and such a very hard cock—

"Hey, lady, move it. Some of us got jobs to go to."

Rebecca's eyes jerked open, her face flushed with heat, even though she knew no one could tell what she'd been thinking, but her voice was firm and in control as she ordered the biggest espresso they made. And a lemon bar.

"LEAVE IT ALONE, OLD MAN."

"I didn't say a word." Mike Donnelly rolled himself out of the path of the coffeemaker.

"I'm in no mood," Jake said, filling his cup for the third time since he'd gotten up.

His father looked at his watch again. Jake knew it was noon. So he'd gone to bed the minute he'd gotten home, what of it. He wasn't missing out on a day of work. And he'd already called to reschedule his physio appointment.

"You're not gonna tell me anything? Not you had a good time, the dinner was crap, nothing?"

"The dinner was great, I had a terrific time and I'm not seeing her again, so what difference does it make?"

"Oh. What happened? She say something?" He leaned forward, his eyes wide. "You say something?"

"No. Neither of us said anything. It was the deal. That's all. It was never going to be more than the one night."

"Oh. So you work these things out ahead of time, huh? Like something in your day planner or your BlackBerry appointment book."

"I don't have a day planner or a BlackBerry. Pa, it's no big deal. It was a setup, we had a nice night. She was...great. Really great. But no more than that."

"Huh."

Jake let out a hell of a sigh. "What?" He sat down at the nook, his thigh killing him. Worth it, though. Every ache and every pain. He'd do it again in a heartbeat. Which wasn't an option.

"You liked her."

"I just said that, yeah."

"No. You *liked* her."

"Dad, you have guests out on the patio. Go play dominoes."

"Pete and Liam, guests? That'll be the day."

"What are you trying to tell me? I've got a headache, and if I have to listen to you any longer, I'm gonna turn around and go right back to bed."

"I'm not trying to tell you anything, big shot. I know my boy, that's all."

Jake squinted at him over the rim of his mug. "Meaning?"

"Sometimes something prearranged can be rearranged. That's all I'm saying."

"You been watching those soap operas again? I'm not looking to rearrange my life."

"Okay, fine. Be that way. I'm going to have lunch with my friends."

"Knock yourself out." Jake sipped his coffee until he was alone in the kitchen. The stupid thing was he did want to see her again. Ridiculous. The two of them, they might have been great between the sheets, on top of the sheets and in the shower, but outside of that, what did they have in common?

Okay, except for film noir. That had been a hell of a surprise, Rebecca loving those old black-and-white movies. She knew a lot about them, too, and yet she hadn't even heard of *Stranger on the Third Floor.* It was the first film-noir thriller, and anybody who loved the genre as much as Rebecca should have that in her collection.

And yeah, she'd been completely interested when he'd told her about the secrets of Manhattan. Lived there her whole life, never knew what was right under her feet. He'd told her a few of the places, like the whispering gallery in Grand Central Terminal and she'd barely scratched the surface of Central Park, especially the Ramble, his favorite spot.

He could hardly believe they'd spent so much time talking last night. The in-betweens had been for refueling, but for two people who'd just met, they'd gotten on like a house on fire. Maybe being naked helped. He'd like to do more of that. Not instead of the sex, because Jesus, that had been spectacular, but he hadn't connected with a woman, with anybody, like that since college.

He finished off his coffee, then got out his phone. He didn't have Kenny on speed dial, but it was close.

"Jake, my man. What's up?"

"You still doing that motorcycle messenger thing?"

"Nah, I'm designing webpages for geeks now."

"You wouldn't want to make a delivery to Midtown for, say, a fifty?"

"When?"

"Now."

Kenny turned off whatever the hell noise had been in the background. "Sure. Why not? The business is just getting started."

Jake knew "the business" was housed in Kenny's grandmother's basement, and if Kenny had a client, it was a relative or someone who owed him money. "Great. See you in ten."

5

ALL THE CAFFEINE IN THE world might have been enough to keep Rebecca from zoning out while she looked at the spreadsheet for donations to date, but she didn't have access. What she did have was about two minutes until Bree would arrive, and that would help.

Brec had already been a friend when Rebecca had decided to play matchmaker between Bree and Charlie, and now that they'd been a couple for almost a month, Bree and Rebecca had gotten even closer.

The best part of Bree was that she made Charlie so very happy. Of all the relatives, and God knew the Winslows did like to procreate, Charlie was the best of thcm. He was also the most notorious, being the editor in chief of *Naked New York,* a blog that virtually everyone in Manhattan depended on to find out what was happening in the city.

It was fascinating to watch the changes her cousin continued to go through during his weird courtship with Bree. He'd been an unswerving commitment-phobe, ready to die on his sword before he'd succumb to a romantic attachment. Until Bree.

Which was one of the big reasons Rebecca had decided to stop actively putting herself out there for dates. It was a very Zen decision. The universe would provide, and in the meantime she'd relax about the whole life-partner thing and enjoy herself with Jake. With men like Jake.

She sneaked yet another glance at his trading card picture, and her sleep-deprived mind went directly to the memory of riding Jake like a rodeo queen. Holy—

"Incoming."

Rebecca jerked at her assistant's voice coming over the intercom. Good. Bree had brought them lunch, including a Red Bull, which would keep Rebecca going for another couple of hours. She had to be on her game today. Every day. Last night had been a horrible lapse in judgment as far as work was concerned. Personally, she had no regrets. It had been the best blind date in her life. One of the hottest dates, period. Just thinking about him made her want to pick up the phone right this—

"Wow, you look like crap," Bree said as she crossed the office. "You must have had an incredible date."

Rebecca ignored the dig because it was completely true and concentrated on her friend. Bree was a tiny thing, maybe five feet, but she carried herself with such panache, dressed herself with so much bravado and flair, that her short stature was always a surprise.

Today she had on superskinny black jeans, four-inch black heels, a white single-button jacket, which was all well and good, but the kicker was the sizzling chartreuse satchel purse and a matching wraparound belt. The outfit was one hundred percent Bree, as was the new do. "Hey, you did stuff to your bangs."

"I did," Bree said. "Little teeny tie-dye at the edges." She put her big purse on Rebecca's desk, then dragged over the wing chair so they could share the space as they shared their lunch. "Wanna see?"

Rebecca stood up and leaned over while Bree did the same. There were at least four colors teasing at the tips, including the brilliant chartreuse, cerise, blue and white. "Fantastic. How long did that take you?"

"Forever." She pulled two Zabar's bags from her purse, a Red Bull, a Dr. Brown's cream soda and a stack of napkins. The unveiling of the meal was done sitting down. Pastrami and Swiss on rye with spicy mustard, a half-dozen dill pickles, a container of potato salad with two plastic forks and, for dessert, four chocolate rugelach.

Rebecca was tempted to start with the cookies; instead, she opened the energy drink.

"So talk to me," Bree said, taking her half of the sandwich and two pickles. "And let me see the card again."

Since the card was already next to her computer keyboard, Rebecca obliged before she grabbed her own food.

"Holy mother of pearl, this guy is so gorgeous I can't stand it." Bree looked up. "Was he even close?"

"Better," Rebecca said, and the sigh that came out after the word made Bree laugh.

"Details, woman."

"He's a cop. Was a cop. Shot, in the line of duty, if you can believe that."

"You're kidding."

"Nope. He wouldn't tell me too much about it, but he was hurt so badly he had the choice of early retirement or a desk job. He retired."

"Where?"

"To the family home, which he's remodeling for his father, who has something. Uh, wait, oh. Rheumatoid arthritis. Poor guy. Nice, though, huh, that Jake's fixing up the house?"

"I meant where was he shot?"

"Oh." Rebecca took a bite of her sandwich before moving on. She was clearly buzzed from the gobs of coffee she'd downed all morning, and now she was giving herself another big dose of caffeine. Eating was no longer optional. She couldn't be flying around the room when her two-o'clock arrived. She ate for a bit, even though she could see Bree was impatient, but finally, she said, "In the shoulder and the thigh."

"Ouch, ouch."

"I'll say. Not that he let it slow him down. Jeez Louise, he's got some stamina. And a killer body."

"Have you ever dated someone like him before?"

"What do you mean?"

Bree took a sip of her soda, then tilted her head to the right. "A blue-collar guy."

Rebecca shook her head. "It made a nice change."

"Did you talk at all?"

"Yes, we talked. What, you think I'm such a snob I can't talk to anyone without an Ivy League degree?"

"It wasn't about you being a snob. I'm wondering if there was any common ground."

Putting down her sandwich for a moment, Rebecca smiled. "We not only had a lot in common, but he was really interesting. Even without discussing his work."

"For example?"

"Films, for one."

"He likes those old black-and-white movies you're so annoying about?"

"A lot, it was— Hey!"

"Sorry to bother," Dani interrupted via the intercom. "But you've got a package."

Rebecca frowned. "It can't wait?"

"It's personal," Dani said. "And I think you're going to want to see it."

"Okay, come on back."

Not a minute later, the office door opened, and there was Dani, looking sharp in her Chanel-inspired suit, her dark hair pinned up in a very sixties chignon. More noteworthy was the vase she held, filled with what looked like a dozen white calla lilies.

Rebecca realized instantly who they were from. That sneak. She hadn't given him her cell number or her work address, although she supposed she was incredibly easy to find. What did it matter? He'd remembered.

"Wow, those are gorgeous," Bree said, as they watched Dani set the glass vase on the end of Rebecca's credenza. "Are they from him?"

"Have to be." Rebecca went around the desk to look for a card.

Dani handed her an oversized envelope. "This came with it."

Suddenly flushed, Rebecca turned just enough that she could see the beautiful flowers and keep her reaction private as she opened the package. God, it would really be embarrassing now if it turned out Jake hadn't been the one to send it, but nope, the moment she saw the DVD cover, she knew. *Stranger on the Third Floor,* starring Peter Lorre.

Jake had been surprised that she didn't own it. With a collection of film noirs like hers, she should have what he referred to as the first "true" example of the genre. The conversation had been as enthusiastic as two punch-drunk disgustingly horny people could manage, especially when one of them was fingering the other blissfully as he spoke. What shocked her even more were the flowers.

"So?" Bree asked from directly behind Rebecca. "What is it? Where did he even find calla lilies? It's still winter."

Rebecca handed her the DVD. "It's from the film," she said, pulling out the note that was still in the envelope.

"Calla lilies are featured in a Peter Lorre picture?"

"*Stage Door.* Katharine Hepburn. They're my favorite flowers."

"Ah," Bree said even as Dani said, "Wow," but Bree went on. "Ten bucks says he wants an encore."

"I'm not taking that bet," Dani said. "Who the hell is this guy?"

Rebecca opened the plain note card.

Hey, Rebecca,
How about we go crazy and try this thing one more time. Dinner? You say when and where?
Jake.

His number followed. That was it. That was enough.

Bree was next to her now, and there was no way she hadn't seen Rebecca's grin or the way her cheeks must still be flushed with pink. "Oh, yeah. You owe me ten bucks," she said. "I like his style. You need to go out with him again."

Rebecca stuffed the note back in the envelope. "Not possible," she said, turning to face her friend. "We'd better finish up eating because I've got a fussy catering manager to deal with at two, and I need more sustenance. And more sugar." She went back to the desk, Bree following.

"No one's gonna tell me, huh?" Dani said. "Fine. No problem. I'm only the minion. I'll go clean the mirrors in the executive lounge or something. That'll be good."

Rebecca's first thought was to make sure Jake's trading card wasn't visible. Not because she didn't want Dani to know; their relationship was a good one, and while they didn't hang out together after work, they did their fair share of girl talk. But hot guys trading cards was like *Fight Club.* The first rule is that you don't talk about it. "He's a nice guy. A friend of a friend. Nothing serious. In fact, it's all in the past tense now."

"Those flowers seem pretty present to me," Bree said. "And a movie with Peter Lorre as The Stranger? That alone is worth at least one more round."

Rebecca took a large bite of sandwich as she sat down, purposefully ignoring the rolling eyes and shaking heads of her friends.

"Does Mr. Nothing Serious have a name at least?"

"Jake," Rebecca said, at the same time as Bree.

"Jake." Dani grinned as she went for the door. "Sounds hot."

That was the problem. He was too hot. And she had a banquet to coordinate and a foundation to run. There was a dinner at NYU she had to attend tonight, then tomorrow night she was going to have a preliminary crack at William West, her primary target for this year's new major donor at yet another fundraiser. The first night she'd even have free was Friday, and by then, if she lived that long, she'd have to pay through the nose to have her hairdresser come to her place so she could work while she was coifed.

It was impossible, that's all. Jake was a one-hit wonder. It was a damn shame, but there it was.

"Would you like something to drink? Coffee? I have some tea, I think, but I'd have to check. But coffee is already made and it's so nice of you to come over." Sally Quayle wrung her hands together. "I get so frightened, what with the news and the stories. Someone was robbed only three blocks away, did you hear? Albert Jester, he was robbed in broad daylight. Drug addicts. They're everywhere. They have no shame, no boundaries."

Jake hadn't had nearly enough sleep to be paying a house call, but he smiled as he gently herded his neighbor toward her kitchen. "Coffee would be nice, thanks. Then we can talk about security. How would that be?"

Sally pressed her hand to her chest as she nodded. "I'll fix you right up. It's freshly brewed, not even fifteen minutes ago."

"I'm sure it'll be great," he said, and he drew out a chair at the table and sat down. Everything still hurt this afternoon and he should have gone back to bed, but he'd never be able to sleep now that he'd sent the DVD to Rebecca. She would call. Why wouldn't she? Even if it was to tell him there wasn't a chance in hell, she wasn't the kind of woman to ignore him. Not after the night they'd had. Besides, she'd thank him for the flowers and the movie. At the very least.

He reached for his cell, twisting his bad shoulder in the process with a move that normally didn't hurt. He needed to make an appointment with Taye, who would read him the riot act while taking great joy in torturing Jake's poor muscles. He had to call soon, too, because lifting that new shower into place? Bending to fix the plaster and the pipes? Not gonna happen until he could move without wanting to punch a hole through a wall.

No calls. Which he already knew. He'd have heard the ring.

"Here you go, Jake." Sally put a big purple mug in front of him, then brought over a little plastic tray that had sugar and milk and a spoon. She took a seat, cradling her own mug in two slightly trembling hands. "My sister's brother-in-law says a Walther PPK pistol is the only way to go. It's what the secret agents use, and spies should know."

Jake put a couple of spoonfuls of sugar in his coffee, then added his milk, thinking about the best approach. She was scared right down to her toes, grieving a death that had happened thousands of miles away, that had to feel completely unreal, and there was no way he was going to let her get her hands on any kind of gun.

"Here's the thing about guns, Sally," he said. "Most people who own guns think they're safe…they figure they can handle anything that comes at them. So they don't bother with the extra dead bolt or the window blocks. And then, if someone does break in, because they've skipped over the houses that have obvious security, the gun owner is so scared, so terrified, either they end up shooting themselves or the perpetrator manages to take the gun from them."

"Oh, but—"

"Sally," he said, lowering his voice, making it as gentle as he could. "The very best way I know of, and remember, I've been a police officer for a long, long time, is to make sure no one ever gets into your house. Ever. We can do that, you and me. I have a friend who's an expert at putting together home security systems that are affordable, but most of all, they're reliable. What do you say we tackle this problem with the best information available, so that you can go to sleep knowing you're safe. Nothing is one hundred percent in this world, but this security system? It's got backups to the backups."

She stared at him for a long while, swallowing enough that he knew she was fighting off tears. Her husband had been a nice man. He shouldn't have died so young, left her on her own. At least she had family. And friends. Living on Howard Street, nobody was too alone, unless they made sure of it themselves, because this was a real neighborhood. As if it had been transported from another era, a time when checking up on one another was like getting groceries. Just something you did.

He took out his wallet, wincing as he moved his damn shoulder again, and brought out a card that had been sitting in there since he'd gotten out of the hospital. He pushed it across the table. "In case you feel the need to talk to someone. This guy? He's a grief counselor and he's supposed to be one of the best. He works with cops, and I've heard he also counsels spies."

Sally's smile told him she wasn't fooled by any of this. But maybe she'd make the call he hadn't been able to. "So what are window blocks?" she asked.

Jake took one last look at his phone, then put it aside as he started explaining the basics.

SHE WAS CRAZY. REBECCA WAS crazy and insane and she should have her head examined. She was also incredibly late, and Jake was going to be here in fifteen minutes, and she hadn't even showered yet.

Rebecca tossed her purse on her bed, kicked her shoes off then dashed to the bathroom, where she started the shower. In record time she'd stripped, put her hair up because there was no time and washed herself from the face down. She'd just shaved this morning, thank God. Shower off, she grabbed her towel and wrapped it around her body as she sat down at the vanity. She'd never done an elaborate job on her makeup except for special occasions and it took her a minute to decide whether tonight's encore presentation counted.

Nope. He'd clearly liked what he'd seen Tuesday night, so she went with the regular. As she smoothed on her blush, she went over what she had to do before he arrived. The plan had been to make dinner together. Homemade pasta with wild mushroom ragout, salad, dessert, the whole nine yards.

That plan had been ditched at four this afternoon, when the orchestra that was set to play for the donor banquet, which was only five days away, had canceled. The reasons were irrelevant, but her schedule, which had included setting out everything so that the actual cooking could be done quickly, had been replaced by her purchase of a very excellent pappardelle with wild mushroom sauce from Felidia in Midtown, and dessert was now a tiramisu agli agrumi. She and Jake would make the salad together. That could be cozy, right?

At the thought of his name, Rebecca shivered. A little frisson that raced from her brain straight down until it made her squeeze her legs together. It had been like that since he'd sent the flowers. No, that wasn't true. It had been like that since she'd sat down at the Kimberly Upstairs bar.

He was terribly distracting at the worst possible time. Every minute her mind wasn't engaged on a specific task, it was on Jake. His hands, the way he'd kissed her, his ass—oh God, that butt was to die for. Unless it was his laugh that stole her attention, or the way his speech quickened when he was talking about the things he loved, like secrets of New York, like films.

She had to get dressed. Now. She finished off her makeup with a couple of swipes of mascara, then a matte lipstick that would stay put. She bent over and shook out her oh-so-straight hair, then flipped it back and done.

Standing in front of the closet wasn't so simple. There were too many choices. Sexy with an eye toward a slower striptease? Something so low-cut the edge of her red lace bra would peek out? Skinny jeans and a loose sweater with mile-high heels?

She went with the loose-fitting but very low-cut pale gray sweater over black skinny jeans with black heels she wouldn't dare wear if she had to walk any real distance.

She had to suck it up to get the jeans zipped, but the package came together well. None of the mirror views were horrible, not even from the rear, and what was she forgetting?

Food, check. Wine. Wine! She rushed to the kitchen and got the bottle of cabernet from the rack. She uncorked it, wishing she'd thought of this before she'd showered, but she'd already planned on giving him some icy-cold vodka for the prep stage. Only one small glass, because neither of them needed to have a hangover, but she knew the vodka would be a hit.

She twirled around her kitchen, the big butcher-block island empty for the moment. Jake was probably minutes away, so she went fast.

First, though, music. A wonderful collection of movie soundtracks, themes from *Laura, Picnic, The Postman Always Rings Twice* and more. Then, the kitchen. The wooden salad bowl came out first, then the cutting board and knife. He said he was bringing everything for the salad, including the dressing. Then she got out plates, bowls, dessert plates, including two trays so they could eat and watch the movie at the same time. Wineglasses came down, and she willed the cabernet to breathe faster because the clock was ticking.

The call from the lobby stopped her halfway between the island and the fridge, where she'd meant to get out the wedge of parmigiana cheese, kicking up her heartbeat. He was here, and she was more nervous than she'd been for the blind date, more nervous than she'd been for her very first date.

She picked up the phone and told the front desk that yes, Mr. Donnelly was expected. She hung up and debated sneaking a quick shot of vodka to calm the hell down. How ridiculous. She already knew the night was going to be great. She'd do her best not to stay up too late because she had to work tomorrow even though it was a Saturday. He already knew what she looked like naked, and he probably couldn't have cared less about her decor or the food or anything but the chemistry they'd already established.

It was one more night. A bonus. That's all. Just for fun.

The bell rang, and she grabbed on to the back of the couch to steady herself before she walked over to the door.

6

JAKE WIPED HIS FREE HAND down his jeans as he waited for Rebecca to open the door. Jesus, the building was incredible. He'd known it would be from the Madison Avenue address, but he'd had no real idea until he'd walked inside. It was a universe away from his old man's house. This was a high-rise with all the bells and whistles, and he couldn't imagine ever having enough money to live there. Only two condos per floor, for God's sake. A concierge. Museum-quality art in the lobby.

He hadn't thought about it much, her being a Winslow. She'd never known anything but luxury and extravagance. He'd met people in her tax bracket before, but they were mostly drug dealers, and there were typically a lot more automatic weapons involved. So his only frame of reference for this kind of life was the movies.

She didn't seem like someone ultrarich. Especially when she was naked and spread for him, pulling him down as she pushed herself into his thrusts.

Maybe he'd try not to greet her with a hard-on, that would be nice. Polite.

She opened the door and one look at her lost him that

battle. Christ, she was even more stunning than he remembered, and he had a great memory.

"Hey," she said, but she was grinning when she said it.

"Hey."

"Come on in."

He took a deep breath and went for it. God damn, but she was something in those heels, in that sweater. It wouldn't bother him at all if they skipped the dinner and went right to dessert.

"You can put that on the island," she said, nodding at the big grocery bag he'd brought. He was in charge of the salad, and he'd spared no expense. That thought made him chuckle as he put the bag down in a kitchen that would have looked at home on the cover of a magazine. With his hands free, he turned back to Rebecca and drew her close. "You're even more beautiful than I remember."

"It's only been three days."

"Extraordinarily more beautiful." He captured her lips in the act of smiling, knew without looking that her cheeks were flushed. She tasted clean and mint fresh, her tongue eager as they kissed as if they'd been apart for weeks.

Her hand moved to the back of his neck, her fingertips sneaking up his scalp, messing his hair and not helping the erection issue at all.

Sadly, she had on far too many clothes, and why were they making dinner when he could have brought a pizza with him? He didn't care about food, not when she was here and there was a bedroom so near.

She was the one to step back, although she paused before she did so. Her eyes were still closed as they breathed each other's breaths. It was all he could do not to close the distance, to take her mouth again and more, but this was her party. As she let go of him, a biting sharp pain shot through his shoulder.

Rebecca cleared her throat, looked over at the island and quickly back at him. “I can hang up your coat.”

He obliged and while she went off to a closet in the foyer, he glanced around. The whole place was like something from *Architectural Digest.* Windows everywhere topped with white, scarlet-edged drapes that didn’t block the view at all. He couldn’t help stepping closer to the window past the dining room table. Spectacular. The Morgan Library was half a block away on 36th Street. When he turned his head to the right, there was the Empire State Building, its tower all lit up.

He then took in the living room. White furniture, white walls with that same brilliant red echoed in the pillows. The area rug was red and white geometric shapes that somehow made everything look cozier instead of just weird. On the wall over the couch was a giant painting, some abstract thing that was mostly deep blue. Not a drop of scarlet in it at all.

It was the kind of classy elegance he could appreciate from a distance. Up close, he had to admit it was intimidating. She was several galaxies outside of his orbit.

His gaze caught on a pair of sneakers half-hidden under a chair by the front door and he breathed easier.

“Vodka?” she asked, and he could tell she was a little nervous, too.

“Depends,” he said, turning to face her. Again, it was like a body blow. A jolt made of desire and heat. “Is it the good stuff?”

“I’ll let you decide,” she said, opening the freezer door. She pulled out a bottle he recognized. Interestingly, it wasn’t the very top of the line. Close, sure, but he had the feeling she was more concerned with liking the drink than impressing him. He hoped so.

She also took out two icy shot glasses, then a small bowl of lime wedges from the fridge. With a steady hand, she rimmed the glasses with the fruit, then poured them each a shot. He picked his up when she lifted hers, and they grinned at each other, which had become an actual thing. Between them. It wasn't something he did with many people, at least not since he'd been a kid.

He clicked her glass. "To second nights."

She nodded. "And calla lilies."

They drank and it went down smooth and cold, leaving him breathless and wanting to taste her again. "Put me to work," he said instead. The war between anticipation and action had moved from his head to his chest. She'd asked him to dinner. It wasn't the same thing as asking him to bed. "I'm good with a knife as long as there's enough room. Not so hot with measuring these days, but I can mix stuff."

"Confession time," she said. "We were going to make pasta. From scratch."

"You do that?"

"When I have time. Which I didn't tonight. So you're going to make me salad while I heat up the rest of dinner. If anyone gets to be the helper, it'll be me."

"It sounds like you've had a hell of a day. I'm decent with a microwave and takeout, unless there's something special about what you brought?"

She smiled at him as she shook her head. "Not a thing." Then she went to the fridge and brought out three different take-out containers. One was filled with pasta, one had a dark mushroom sauce and one she didn't open.

He located everything he'd need, particularly the wine, which he poured. He handed her a glass. "Sit down, relax, watch me tear lettuce to shreds. I like the music, by the way."

She inhaled deeply, let it out slowly, but rather than moving to the chair at the end of the island, she leaned in and kissed him. "Thank you. Work has been brutal."

When Rebecca turned, he could see a hint of red at the edge of the low-cut neckline. Like the edges of the curtains, the pillows on the couch. He was going to enjoy peeling away her layers.

He brought out his salad kit. Not that it was anything so studied or interesting. Four kinds of lettuce because according to his old friend Sal's mother only savages ate a salad with only romaine. Green onions were next, red peppers, cherry tomatoes, green olives, black olives and finally fresh basil from Sal's mother's kitchen window. Then came the grapeseed oil and balsamic vinegar he'd mixed up ahead of time, and finally, a lemon. He washed his hands, dried them on an incredibly soft kitchen towel, then went to work tearing lettuce as he stared at the gorgeous woman with the bared shoulder.

The sight was enough to make him thankful he hadn't picked up a knife yet. Her sweater had fallen to reveal one red bra strap across pale, perfect skin. Her legs in those tight black jeans were spread, one of her hands resting on the edge of her chair between her thighs. She raised a glass of dark wine to her lips and drank. When he was able to wrest his gaze from her lips, he found her staring at him, her pupils dark behind the fringe of bangs and eyelashes.

"How's the wine?" he asked, amazed his voice didn't break and that he'd said actual words.

"Good," she said. "Not as good as watching you manhandle that lettuce."

"The lettuce had it coming." He tore the last of the radicchio and picked up the escarole. "It must be demanding, running such a large foundation."

"It can be," she said, nodding as if the mere mention had reminded her again how exhausted she was. "Especially this week. I have no business doing this tonight."

"Why not? A girl's gotta eat."

She half smiled. "If that's all we're going to do tonight, then I think we need to have a talk."

"No, that's not all. But maybe we should postpone the movie."

She stilled, blinked at him.

Her reaction brought it home, what he'd suggested. This wasn't supposed to continue. Tonight was a one-off, a thank-you, he imagined, for the flowers and the DVD. "Or not."

She swallowed, even though she hadn't had any more wine. "No, that's a nice idea. The movie would be better if it happened after Wednesday night. After Thursday night, honestly, so I can finally get a decent night's sleep."

"What happens on Wednesday?"

"Big dinner. Huge dinner. It's where I flatter the hell out of our regular donors and woo the potentials. This year there's one very big fish I'm determined to land. He seems interested, but he's also playing coy. Teasing me along. But it'll be worth it. His contribution would end up in the tens of millions over the length of the endowment. That's game-changing money. That's schools and loans and medicine and lives saved. So many lives."

"No wonder you're exhausted. That's got to be a lot of pressure."

"Some things are worth it."

"I've always thought so."

"Hell, you were willing to put your life on the line. Talk about pressure."

He looked around the kitchen until he found the big chef's knife, then turned back to his salad and Rebecca. "Different kind, but yeah. Pressure was part of it. Not as much as deciding who gets what resources. That's tough. For everyone who gets, there are probably dozens, hundreds who don't."

She shifted on her chair, although thankfully she didn't adjust her sweater. He had to be careful because of the knife, but every chance he could, he'd look at that red strap, then her face. Holy shit.

"I don't have to make all those decisions," she said. "We have a board of directors. My job is to first make sure we're always refreshing our coffers and then to narrow down the choices of how we want to spend the money. So many need so much, it's not easy."

"I'll bet. I imagine you take into account what other groups are doing, try to spread the wealth?"

She nodded. "It's a triage system. Short- and long-term goals. Maximum benefit for the greatest number of people, things that hopefully turn out to be more than quick fixes. But I'd rather hear about your house and your father. You're doing a complete remodel?"

He grinned, thinking about what his dad would say walking into this joint. "Nope, just giving him living space on the ground floor. He has trouble with the stairs."

"You do a lot of that DIY stuff?"

"Nope. Learning as I go. Turns out the internet is a pretty useful thing. And DVDs. Lots of how-to DVDs." He finished the last of the chopping, put the salad together except for the dressing. He opened the containers of food, dividing the pasta and sauce between the two big plates.

Her hand on his shoulder made him jump. How had he not heard those heels click? Jesus, how rapidly his self-preservation instincts were devolving.

"I'll get this part," she said, so close to him that he felt the heat of her breath on his jaw.

Fast as that, he was all about Rebecca. The dinner could vanish for all he cared because her hand was still warm on his shoulder and her hip was pressing against him. He had his arms around her before he finished turning, his mouth on hers a second later.

Tasting her was better than anything on the menu. It was intimate and slow, their kiss, and maybe because he knew they were going to stop, that he wasn't going to drag her to the bedroom right this second, he paid attention to what was happening here, what he had.

She tasted like Rebecca. Jesus, how it compressed his chest to realize he knew that taste, could have picked her out of a crowd blindfolded. And while there were a dozen different places he wanted to memorize with his tongue, for now he slicked and slid against her in a slow back-and-forth, deep and shallow. Everything was what he wanted of this small, amazing part of her. Lips, tongue, teeth, breath, heat, wet.

He'd pushed his hips against her and it was the shock wave that brought him back to the room, to dinner. He pulled away, but only because he knew he would have her again soon.

SOMEHOW, REBECCA MANAGED to slow her heartbeat and stop her shaking long enough to heat up the entrée. Jake's salad was fantastic, and she ate more of that than the pasta. He did the reverse, so that worked out. The bottle of wine was almost finished and dessert waited, but Rebecca wasn't terribly interested in dessert.

"I could make coffee," he said. "There's that last box out on the counter."

She put down her wineglass and stood. "That's tiramisu, if you want some. Or we could just go back to my bedroom."

He looked up at her, and she almost laughed at the way his entire expression said there was no contest. "Where's the bedroom?" he asked, taking her hand in his, bringing it to his lips, where he kissed her palm.

"A hundred miles away."

He rose, pulled her into his body. "The couch isn't."

She shook her head, letting her lips brush his as she did. "Want you in my bed."

"Take me there."

It wasn't easy, letting go of him. So she didn't. She just slid her fingers into the waistband of his jeans and tugged him along, moving faster with each step and each thought of what came next.

The moment she crossed the threshold of her bedroom, her shoes were history. He was pulling up her sweater before she could get her hand out of his pants. They each worked on unbuttoning and unzipping, but he won the race by a mile. And then he tugged down, hard, pulling her jeans and her panties down to her knees.

"Oh, God," he said, and he ran his hands up the front of her thighs.

"Wait, wait. Do your shirt. I can't—"

"I don't care about my shirt. We have to get rid of your pants."

"I'm trying!"

"You suck at it." He batted her fumbling fingers away,

and they concentrated on divesting themselves of their own clothes. She shed her pants; his shirt had disappeared by the time she looked up, but when she reached behind her back to undo the clasp of her bra, he said, "Wait. Don't. Stop."

"Don't stop? Or Don't. Stop?"

"Leave it on." Then his trousers and boxer briefs hit the floor; his cock was as perfectly hard as she remembered. He whipped off his undershirt so swiftly he couldn't hide the wince as he stressed his shoulder.

He pressed up against her, his ability to control his hips apparently gone with his clothes, which she found extremely sexy.

After a kiss that nearly missed her mouth completely, he was pushing her backward toward the bed. "Sit," he said.

She did, wondering what he was up to.

It turned out he was going down on his knees. She worried for a moment, but he didn't seem to be in any pain, although she doubted he could kneel long. Then he had his hands on her knees, spreading her wide.

"Watch me," he said. His voice was unraveling. How much did she love that?"

He kept his gaze on hers as he bent forward. Her bed was high, and she had a nice view of the moment Jake switched his attention from her face to his new objective. Beginning with his lips on her inner thigh. Lips and tongue, a wicked combination. Hands and fingers, too, so that there was sensation all along the pathway to her pussy.

She wanted to press her legs together, but she couldn't, so she squeezed what was available. Jake must have noticed because he moaned low and long as he picked up the pace.

Finally, his hot breath painted her labia, and then, softly, he licked her from the bottom of her cleft to the top.

JAKE LOST HIMSELF IN THE taste of her, in the salt on his tongue, in the scent. His fingers spread her open, and he went to town. It was gorgeous, and she was amazing, and he'd loved every second of what she tasted like and the sounds she made when he pointed his tongue and fucked her with it.

Her hand was in his hair, and when he hit pay dirt, she let him know. His thigh hurt, but it was so worth it. The sad part was that he couldn't just move in, stay for the night. His cock was insistent, but his wound wouldn't leave him be, so he kept his tongue hard and pointed and worked fast on her full, hard clit.

That brought her other hand into his hair, and if he was half-bald at the end of this, well, hair grew back.

Her thighs pressed against his ears as her moans got louder, and when she started chanting his name, he went into fifth gear.

It was a race to see if he would suffocate or she would come first.

He lived.

It was a damn good thing she had the condom at the ready, because about one hot minute later, he was on the bed. He'd flipped her over so she was on her hands and knees, and he went to heaven as he thrust inside her.

She dropped to her elbows, her head on her pillow, and he'd never seen anything so erotic in his life. So proper on the outside, so cool and collected. In here, with him, wanton, abandoned and the sexiest thing alive. But dammit, he was going to come too fast. It's what she did to him.

He gripped her too tightly, his cock pistoned hard, hard, and he was swearing in his head because he couldn't even speak.

He meant to turn her over, to look her in the eyes, maybe kiss her as they came, but that would have to happen later because Rebecca stole a lot more than his composure. He came as if he'd never done it before, as if he'd do anything to be with her again.

7

THE ALARM WENT OFF AT the unholy hour of five, purposefully shrill. Rebecca threw her arm over to stop the beeping, but there was no way Jake could have slept through that. No one in a three-mile radius could have.

"That was..." Jake didn't finish the sentence.

"It's the only thing that gets me up. I just sleep through music or anything that doesn't make me want to rip out my ears."

"Next time, we're doing this on a weekend you don't have to work."

She turned over, kicking the duvet into something less restricting. They'd certainly been energetic last night. Despite her tiredness. At least they'd gotten five hours of sleep. "Next time?"

He turned to her, and while the draw was there, as urgent as it had been every time she got a look at him, they both played by morning-breath rules. "I keep doing that, don't I?"

She nodded. "Evidently, I don't mind."

"Excellent."

"I'm going to take a lot longer than you in the bathroom," she said. "Feel free to shower. There's a fresh toothbrush in the drawer under the rolled-up towels."

"I was kind of hoping for an in-home demo."

She brushed the back of her fingers across his cheekbone. "That would be a terribly risky thing to do."

"We're modern-day warriors," he said. "I have every faith."

Her laughter made her cover her mouth and start the day off better than she could have hoped. "Not when it comes to resisting you."

He hummed happily and planted his forehead against her chest above her breasts. His hand started petting her, long slow strokes that made what she had to do next very difficult.

"You have to get out of my bed."

"Harsh," he said, his sleep-roughened voice muffled.

"Vigilance is my only hope."

He sniffed. Moved himself back to the safe side of the bed. "Fine. I'll get out of your bed. I'll use your new toothbrush. But just know that I plan to make you a great omelet for when you've finished getting ready."

She laughed again. "Is that your idea of a threat?"

"Yeah, it's pretty weak. But it's all I've got. Too damn early in the morning." He threw back the covers and stood, his body still gorgeous, but she could see that some parts moved quicker than others. How much did those wounds hurt him every single day? She wished there was more to be done.

His cock certainly hadn't been affected. He was half-hard, and she knew it wouldn't take much to get him to attention. But work wasn't going anywhere. The thought of all she had to do today made her moan.

He walked to the end of the bed and collected his

clothes from the settee. "Anything you don't like in an omelet?"

She shook her head. "Everything in my fridge is fair game. Whatever you make will be wonderful. Oh, and the coffee should be ready in about five minutes."

He grinned and that quiver came back to her tummy. As she watched his butt while he walked to the bathroom, she wondered if she was being a complete idiot about all this. Letting him make her breakfast. Implying there'd be a next time. She was always careful about making friends too quickly, letting herself get too close. But kicking him out of her bed was hard enough. She just wasn't ready to kick him out of her life.

JAKE TOOK THE SUBWAY BACK to Brooklyn. It wasn't that crowded early on a Saturday morning so he was able to stretch out his leg. Of course, he did what he always did: scoped out the exits, every passenger who was in his car. Looked for signs of inebriation, of dilated pupils, of anything hinky. Then a sweep of the clothes, the hoodies in particular, the jeans. Possible weapon or cell phone? A loner paying too much attention to another passenger? It wasn't something he planned, it was the way he was. It didn't matter that he didn't have the badge, his brain had wired itself to the job. He never sat with his back to a wall, he always knew where the exits were, he was conscious of body language and facial ticks. A lot of good it did him now. Not only was he stuck with permanent injuries, he could also look forward to a lifetime of paranoia.

He was gonna have to get a little more serious about therapy if he wanted to keep up with Rebecca. And not just physical therapy.

He shook his head at his foolishness. Truth was, he

was playing with fire. Walking into that building last night had shown him everything he needed to know about him and Rebecca. Yeah, it was all fun and games and getting naked, but they'd also done a lot of other stuff. Stuff that didn't come with the normal one-night-stand package. Talked, for one thing. Talked a lot. Laughed. He'd cooked for her. She'd…opened wine.

He stared at the dark tunnel outside the subway window, everything speeding by. He would go home today, keep working on the downstairs bathroom. Listen to a ton of bad cop jokes. Watch his old man struggle to hold his fork, his mug, a domino. And parts of his body would burn angry at how he'd moved and strained and pushed too hard. But the other parts, the center of him, was glad he'd wrecked himself with Rebecca Thorpe, even if it never occurred to her that he might feel uncomfortable in a bed that cost more than he'd make in a year. Past tense. Made in a year.

Now, shit, disability. There was the house, eventually, but not for a long time, please God. And he had some savings. But he couldn't take her out to the type of places she was used to. Meals at some of those joints ran to the thousands. He could barely imagine what food could be worth that. Even with wine.

She was used to dealing in billions, he was looking for bargains at Greschlers' Hardware. He understood the part where they were naked, the sweaty part. He was having trouble with the talking. With liking her the way he did.

He rocked to the side at the curve, then settled. Being an undercover cop, being in with people who'd shoot him if he so much as looked at them funny, he'd learned to read people. It was survival, and it didn't go away once he was off the job. Rebecca liked him. She was comfortable with him, and she wanted him to like her back.

The women he'd been involved with, they were all people whose lives he understood. If they weren't from his neighborhood, they were from one just like it. Pizza from the corner was a fine meal, getting together for some green beer and corned beef on St. Paddy's Day, watching Notre Dame at the corner bar. That's what he knew. Not that he was embarrassed by his home or his life, not at all. But it had given him his perspective. His frame of reference.

Rebecca didn't fit outside of the bedroom. No two ways about it. He didn't understand her motives, and that could be a problem. Motives were important.

Hell, he barely understood why he was pushing this thing, asking for more when it should have ended. He might have come from a long line of cops, but he wasn't just some mook who didn't understand what was what. Until her. Until Madison Avenue and fucking wild mushroom ragout, for Christ's sake. What were they trying to prove? Was he her good deed for the year? Her attempt to get to know the little people? Was she his last-ditch attempt to prove he was still all man and not just an unemployed cripple?

The train slowed, and he looked up, saw he had four stops to go. But he watched the doors as they opened, scanned the small groups of people as they entered, chose seats. A couple of gangbangers sat front and center, so Jake would keep his wits about him, but he didn't expect anything to happen. Except a train ride back to his real life.

He'd think about her, no question there. And he'd see her again, if he could figure out how to meet on neutral territory. Not his place, because jeez, the old man? Pete? Liam? They'd trip all over themselves trying to impress her. But he didn't feel right about going back to her place. Wouldn't, until he figured some things out. Like why he was already counting the minutes until he could be with her again.

REBECCA CLICKED THE TEXT function on her cell phone, clicked again on Bree's name and typed:

Donate my body to science

Not five seconds later, Bree responded:

Don't tell me you're still wrking

I will never not be wrking Bree. NEVER!

It'll get better. Tell me re BLUE EYES. Was 2nd as good as 1st?

He made me salad. Omelet this am. Yum. In every sense of the word.

Rebecca leaned back in her chair as she eyed the report spread out on her desk. She'd paused the demo that was currently on her screen and tried to get through the first page of the report three times, but she kept losing the thread. Thank God, the beep that told her Bree had texted her back saved her.

OMG. I can't stand it. U HAVE to invite him!

To what?

The donor dinner. Duh.

Rebecca blinked at the text, the message not fully computing for a full minute. She wasn't going to invite Jake to the donor dinner. He'd feel horribly out of place. Although she would certainly prefer sitting next to him rather than her cousin Reggie, not so affectionately known as Peckerhead, at least by Rebecca and Charlie. She took a sip of coffee before she set to typing again.

I can't invite him. Awkward.

For who?

Him!

Really? CW

Hey, who let you into this convo?

Sorry, he read over my shoulder. Stole my phone. I've slugged him.

Charlie, go away.

Is he a porn star? A gigolo? Missing teeth, perhaps? CW

Bite me.

Rebecca started typing instantly, before Charlie could get a text in edgewise.

It's not his kind of thing.

Says U. Ask.

Yeah, ask. I'm still betting missing teeth. Front uppers. CW

If I'd wanted a pain in the ass relative, I'd have had a brother. I have to go back to work.

Think about it. CW

Rebecca got out of her text screen and put her phone in her right-hand drawer. She glanced at the report, but didn't linger. Her mind was far too occupied by the notion of inviting Jake to the banquet. The idea had grown roots during that brief, weird conversation. Not all of them pleasant.

Jake in a tuxedo? That she could deal with. In fact, she wanted to see that very, very badly. Something tailored, fitting those broad shoulders and tapering to his waist. Black, almost traditional, but perhaps a hint of cerulean blue in his cuff links? It would have to be subtle, not even his pocket kerchief, a mere spot of blue. Maybe Burberry or Tom Ford, definitely single button and razor-sharp lapels.

She realized she was smiling when she reached for her coffee, but the grin faded quickly. What would an ex-policeman from Brooklyn do with a Tom Ford tux? The people she was hosting, these were men and women used to every luxury the world had to offer, and the most casual among them knew who was and wasn't one of them.

She'd grown up among the highest of the classes, and as much as their excesses bothered her, she had to be careful lest she not include herself. Just because she made it her mission to spread the wealth of the Winslow Foundation to a much broader and less-fashionable base, she didn't exactly live an ascetic's life. Her home was worth over three million dollars and that was just the space. She considered it a long-term investment, a clever buy at a time when the economy had taken a dive. But it was also what she was accustomed to.

She'd never lived in a building without a doorman. Never *had* to work. Her salary at the foundation was put right back into play as a donation, partly for the tax benefits, mostly to compensate for the guilt. It was convenient to think she was being generous when in truth, she could live extraordinarily well for the rest of her life on her trust fund. As it was, she barely touched the principal.

Her cup was almost empty, and she walked to the private lounge in a daze of sleep deprivation and hazy discomfort. Bree had come into her life, and therefore into Charlie's life, as a result of another pang of elitism. Rebecca had been invited to the lunch exchange by a professor she knew from NYU who no longer belonged to the group. They'd originally met in the park. Rebecca had never told Grace her last name, although she was fairly certain the English prof had recognized her. Grace had probably thought she was offering a chance for humility. Looking back, Rebecca agreed that she had.

Bree never spoke about it, about the disparity between their lifestyles. Rebecca imagined she and Charlie had talked. Knew they had, because he'd been so very famous as the creator and editor in chief of *Naked New York*. He was a celebrity in his own right, one who had used his wealth and influence to build his singular empire, one that had shouted clearly and loudly that he wasn't one of "those" Winslows.

As she poured a fresh cup of coffee, she thought about herself and Charlie, how they'd been so close growing up. Uncomfortable with the trappings of their heritage, but not enough to walk away, not completely. In Charlie's case, he'd replicated the success and influence, but in his own style. In hers, she'd decided to use her power for good. Going to law school had been hard, but worth it, as had learning everything she could about running a foundation and fundraising. Her sacrifices were tiny. Miniscule. Complaining about any of it unforgivable.

Which brought her in a roundabout way back to Jake and the question of his invitation. Once at her desk, she took out her purse and pulled out his trading card. God, he was ridiculously handsome, but his looks weren't what attracted her most now that she knew him. Maybe Charlie and Bree had been right to question her easy dismissal. Because it had been a knee-jerk reaction, that immediate no. Not, she realized, out of the goodness of her heart and concern for Jake.

She was honestly too tired to be having an existential crisis about her entire life. In another hour, she'd leave, go straight home to her mansion in the sky and put herself to bed. Tomorrow, when her brain wasn't packed with cotton, she'd think again.

"OKAY, HIT ME," JAKE SAID, taking a deep breath and letting his aggravation at being walkie-talkied to death wash over him like a passing breeze.

"What did the cop say to his belly button?"

"I don't know, Dad. What did the cop say to his belly button?"

"You're under a vest!"

Jake shook his head as he listened to the laughter coming from the front porch. After thirty or so seconds, he figured his old man was finished for the moment, and he could release the button. At least this joke hadn't made him groan. And where the hell they kept coming up with the vile things, Jake had no idea. He'd have guessed the internet, but not a one of them had a computer, or a cell phone with Wi-Fi. As for listening to anyone long enough to learn how to turn any internet-related device on, forgetaboutit. Stubborn old goats.

But, what the hell. He was something of a Luddite himself when it came right down to it. His needs were simple; he didn't have to have every new gadget that came down the pike. His laptop wasn't new, but it let him watch DVDs, get the scores, read the headlines and, from time to time, he'd even streamed a feature film. The screen was too small to make a habit of that last one, but it had come in handy when he'd been recuperating. Walking had been a real pain for quite some time, but as long as he had the laptop close, he didn't die of boredom. He was especially grateful for online books. They'd gotten him through some tough days.

Now, though, he wished like hell he'd never started this remodeling job. Putting up tile had to be the most tedious job in the world. It had all looked simple on paper but, as he couldn't escape learning, there was a great difference between remodeling and remodeling well. The bane of his existence wasn't the repetitive motions or the heavy lifting, even though those aggravated his wounds, it was the level. He could never tell when that water bubble was straight. He'd even sprung for one with a laser, and he still had trouble.

It made him long for the days of hiding in plain sight, hanging with drug dealers and fearing every breath would be his last.

The dreaded beep from the walkie-talkie interrupted his self-pity and he clicked on the button. "Got another one so soon?"

"Nope. Not quite."

It was Liam. Liam, who hardly ever used the walkie-talkie.

"We could use some help down here."

"What's wrong?" Jake dropped the trowel onto the tarp at his feet and hurried down the hallway, his senses on overdrive. He ignored the burn in his thigh as he raced through the living room to the front door. Throwing the door open, he saw the problem, and he had to stop himself from just lunging to his father, who was sprawled awkwardly on the sidewalk directly in front of the stairs that led up to the porch. He hadn't made the turn. It had happened once before, and Jake had promised to extend the porch but his dad had refused, insisted they would just move the damn card table they played on, move it back so he had more room.

"He's okay," Pete said. "I caught the chair before it hit his head."

Jake didn't see any blood. Liam was bent over, holding Mike's head in his big pale hands.

"I'm fine. Don't panic." Mike waved his crooked hand at Jake as if he was being a bother, and the way he glared at Liam it was clear the old moron hadn't wanted Jake to know.

Jake got down the steps faster than he had in weeks and squatted by his dad. "Anything hurt?"

"Yeah, my ego. Stupid ass wheelchair. I need to get me one of those sporty ones, the kind they race with."

"Yeah, that's exactly what you need." He put his arm behind his father's shoulders, the right arm because there was no way to use his left, not for this, not when a failure would matter so much. Screw it if the whole shower broke into a million pieces. Not this.

Liam helped, and together, they made one reasonably strong person able to lift Mike to his feet. The terrible claw of his hand grabbed on to Jake's upper arm, and while it hurt him, it had to be fiercely painful for his father.

"Come on. Let's get you in the chair you've got. See if it still works."

His dad nodded and took one unsteady step while Jake looked at him with every ounce of his attention. He didn't seem to be favoring anything more than usual, and he wasn't bleeding that Jake could see. But he'd still make an appointment with the doctor, get Mike checked over. So far, none of his spills had done anything too damaging, but it scared Jake to the bone each time it happened.

Whatever his own future held, it would include full-time care for his father. Maybe that would be Jake's job, and maybe it would last until he grew too old to get upstairs himself, but that was okay. He'd have plenty of breaks and time for himself, because they lived on Howard Street, in Windsor Terrace, and they were surrounded by a community who gave a shit when it counted.

Pete brought the wheelchair down the ramp, but not right up to Mike, which was good because Jake needed to watch him for a few more steps. Then they pushed him up. Pete and Liam did. The bastards slipped themselves into place, not giving Jake an option.

He could have made it up the ramp, goddammit, but it would have been a strain. He wasn't the man he used to be, not when it came to ramps or doing the job he was born to do or making love to a beautiful woman. He was a different Jake now, but the reality and his self-perception were still at war. Time, his physiotherapist had said. He had to give it time—

His cell rang, and as he limped up the steps after the old men, he put it to his ear. "Hello."

"Jake."

He paused, one foot on the porch. He felt a rush of heat down his back, settling low. "Rebecca."

"This is completely rude and please feel absolutely free to say no, but I'm actually in Brooklyn. Not far from your place, and I was wondering if you'd mind if I dropped by."

Every bit of his cop's instinct said it was a bad idea. Jake himself looked like a poor excuse for a day laborer. His father seemed to be okay now, but he'd be in a lot of discomfort and there was every possibility that seeing Rebecca Winslow Thorpe show up on his doorstep would be the final straw that did him in, and the house looked like shit. Not to mention Pete and Liam were about as tactful as three-year-olds. "Sure," he said, and with one word, he was doomed. "You know the address?"

"Well, yes. I know, creepy, but Google."

"It's okay. Come on over. Just be aware, you're gonna get what you get."

"That's all I want," she said. "I can be there in ten. Unless… I'm standing not five feet from Luigi's Pizza, which seems to be popular, given the crowd. I could bring one? Maybe some beer?"

Jake shook his head, more at the weird way this day was going than her offer. It was almost five, and he hadn't given a thought to dinner, knowing he'd either scrounge or they'd have something delivered. Rebecca didn't need to come with food, but as surreal as it was that she had called at all, it was also pretty brave, and she'd probably feel more comfortable if she came bearing gifts. "That'd be great, except there's four of us. My old man, his buddies, me. So how about you tell Gio behind the counter that the Donnellys need a couple pies and he can put it on our tab. Tell him to deliver 'cause it's gonna take him a little while if I know Sunday night at Luigi's. I got the beer covered, but if you want anything fancier than that, you're on your own."

She laughed. "I'll see you soon."

He clicked off, stared at his phone for a minute before he put it in his pocket. This was not his life.

8

REBECCA HAD ARRIVED IN picturesque Windsor Terrace, Brooklyn, at four-fifteen. Delivered by cab to what she guessed was the middle of town. It was certainly a busy street. Lots of people walking, businesses booming. Well, that was an exaggeration, if you didn't count Luigi's and the nearby bar.

But there were people on the streets moving at a pace that wasn't close to the speed of Manhattan, and there were families with strollers, dogs on leashes, dogs off leashes. Groups of teenagers, a startling number of whom were accessorized with not only tattoos, although those were plentiful, but metal. Industrial-looking rings embedded in earlobes, some stretching the skin so much it made her cringe. She couldn't help thinking of the long-term effects, but then that must be either a sign of her age, or that she was even more rigid and conservative than she'd thought.

The likelihood of her reaction coming from her class bias was mostly the reason she'd come to Brooklyn in the first place. After a long overdue excellent night's sleep, she'd continued to be bothered by the idea that she hadn't even considered asking Jake to be her date for the banquet.

After she'd run through all the reasonable issues—the fact that they didn't know each other that well outside of the bedroom, that they weren't technically dating and that he'd probably be bored out of his mind even if he did agree to go—she'd been left with a giant bundle of uncomfortable doubt. She honestly had no idea if she'd discounted him because she was being thoughtful or prejudiced.

It had taken her over an hour of walking up and down the big street to finally give in and call him, even though she was still confused and unsure. She could be calling him out of liberal guilt. She could be wanting him there because she liked him. What if it was both? What then?

No answers yet, but the deciding factor had been the pleasure she felt when she thought about him sitting next to her. Being able to look into his amazing blue eyes when she felt overwhelmed.

It was a novel sensation, liking him the way she did. Normally her turn-ons were more cerebral and practical. She liked brains, business acumen, elegance, good taste and a liberal bent. A sense of humor was a non-negotiable must-have, although difficult to find in combination with the rest of her requirements.

Jake was clever and he had a broad scope of interests. He made her laugh. She had no idea about the rest and hadn't cared that she hadn't known. Because he was for sex. Only, that wasn't how it was turning out.

She had arrived at the corner of Howard Street. One left turn, a few blocks, and she'd be there, at Jake's home. She'd meet his father. See the work Jake was doing on the house. There would be no sex involved. And while she was pretty sure she was going to ask him to be her date Wednesday night, she was leaving that option open.

The pizzas would arrive in the next ten or so minutes, according to Gio, who turned out to be the owner, so she should get a move on and stop stalling. Turning left, she looked at the row houses lining the wide street. The homes were virtually identical except for the front porches, which were wide and uniquely decorated, mostly with furniture that wouldn't be damaged by snow yet could be heavily used in more temperate months. She liked them, each of them, some with religious statues, some with art that gave a great deal away about the owners. The big old front porches were unheard of in Manhattan and she wondered what it would be like to grow up in a place like this.

The whole neighborhood felt as if it was from another era, and from what little she'd read about it in her Google searches, that was the point. The folks who lived here protected the ambience, and while they couldn't slow the gentrification of the main thoroughfares, they could maintain the residential streets in their old-fashioned glory.

She was nearing his place, and she hesitated again, her hands buried in the deep pockets of her thick wool coat, her boots clicking on the bumpy sidewalk and her nervous heart signaling her flight-or-fight response.

There were men on the porch, sitting at a card table. Old men, gray-headed and wrinkled, laughing at something. They weren't looking for her or even glancing in her direction. Jake hadn't told them? Okay. Fair enough, he knew the players.

She wasn't naive enough to think these men wouldn't know who she was. They would also have opinions about her family, and she would bet those opinions weren't favorable. The Winslows were not well-known for their charity and kindness despite the foundation.

She took another few steps and the laughing dimmed. The one with the most hair, the one facing her, had grown quiet. Seconds later, the two other men turned, making no effort whatsoever to hide their blatant curiosity.

She doubted they'd arrived at the Winslow part yet, but they would certainly know she was an outsider. "Hello," she said, smiling as she reached the front steps of the row house. "I'm here to see Jake."

"You are, huh?" The man who spoke was Jake's father. The one who'd spotted her first. This close, she could see he was in a wheelchair, see his gnarled hands. His accent, even with three small words, was epic.

"Yes, sir. He's expecting me."

"Then you'd better come on up," he said.

At the top of the steps, the appeal of the porch was made vividly clear. The large space heater did a terrific job of keeping out the bitter chill. She imagined only big storms would keep these troopers indoors. The card table was strewn with dominoes and coffee mugs, a couple of pens and a pad of paper. There were walkie-talkies, not cell phones, in front of each man, which must be their intercom system, a way to get Jake outside pronto.

The man sitting next to Jake's father raised his walkie-talkie to his mouth. "Jake."

"Yeah, Pete?" came the reply a few seconds later.

"Your friend is here."

"I'll be right out."

God, how they were staring. She felt a blush on her cheeks that made her even warmer. "I'm Rebecca

Thorpe," she said. "I was in the neighborhood, and Jake said it was all right if I came by."

"You come to this neighborhood often?" This from the biggest of the three, the one who had to twist around to see her. He had phenomenally bushy eyebrows.

"No. Never before today. It's a great street."

"We like it," Jake's father said, and it looked as if he was about to say more when the front door opened.

Jake wore jeans and a plaid flannel shirt, both looking as if they'd been with him a long time. She closed her hand into a fist to fight the urge to touch him, even though he was standing all the way across the porch. The tool belt hanging on his hips seemed a little newer than his clothes and the ensemble was surprisingly sexy. She couldn't hold back her grin, and neither, it seemed, could he. "You found it."

"I did."

"Gio give you any trouble?"

"Nope. But he also wouldn't tell me what kind of pizzas he was sending. I hope I didn't just get two pineapple and ham pies because that would be—"

"A travesty," he said, interrupting. "No. No pineapples have ever touched a pizza in this house."

"Okay, then. I guess I'll stay for a bit."

"Good."

Jake's father coughed. Loudly, and completely fake.

His son startled at the sound, as if he'd forgotten the old men were there. "Everybody, this is Rebecca. Thorpe."

"We know," his dad said.

"Ah. Recognized her, huh?"

"No, she had the manners God gave a child of five and introduced herself."

Jake, in the manner of kids from every walk of life,

rolled his eyes. "Rebecca, I'd like you to meet my father, Mike Donnelly, the emperor of Howard Street. To his left is family friend and classic car enthusiast Pete Baskin. The third gentleman is also an old family friend, Liam O'Hara. If you need any information about any of the *Die Hard* movies, he's your man."

"It's lovely to meet all of you, and I hope I haven't disturbed your game too much."

"Liam's cheating, anyway," Pete said at the exact same time Mike said, "Pete's cheating."

No one but Rebecca seemed to be surprised, but it made her laugh.

"Who's up for something to drink?" Jake asked. "The pizza should be arriving any minute."

Pete and Liam wanted beer, Mike coffee.

Jake held out his arm, inviting Rebecca into the house.

"Don't you hide her away in there, Jakey. We'll be wanting to talk to this beautiful young lady."

"Yes, Dad. I promise not to let her make a clean getaway."

"Hey, Rebecca," Pete said. "How many cops does it take to throw a man down the stairs?"

Jake groaned as all three men at the table smiled broadly, their wrinkles framing their grins like theater curtains.

"I don't know. How many?"

Pete laughed even before he said, "None. He fell."

The old men laughed. Hard. Full of wheezes and a couple of hiccups, it was impossible not to laugh with them. When she got a load of Jake's grimace, it all became funnier.

As she passed Jake and entered the house there was

no doubt she was not a native of this strange land, but a visitor on a guest pass.

The hallway was short, a little dark and had no photographs or flowers, only a place to hang coats and another to stash boots. Jake helped her off with her big wool monstrosity and hung it up, but he didn't ask her to remove her boots.

The front room was old-fashioned with a wooden fireplace, flowered wallpaper and a staircase leading to the second floor. There was a very nice hardwood floor. The furniture looked cozy with tables close at hand for cups or magazines. No TV though, but that mystery was cleared up when she was escorted into the living room. But before she could look around, Jake stepped close and pulled her into a kiss that went from welcome to "hi, there" in thirty seconds.

The flannel felt wonderful beneath her hands, or maybe that was knowing it was Jake she was touching. Unable to resist, she explored his manly tool belt and copped a grab of his ass for good measure.

He laughed as he kissed her, which was one heck of a nice thing.

When she drew back, she found his gaze, those blue eyes doing strange and wondrous things to her body. "I never just show up," she said. "Never. My entire family, including all my ancestors, are appalled. It's the height of rudeness."

"Boy, are you not from this neighborhood. No one calls ahead. They just barge the hell in, no matter what. It's a pain in the ass."

"It's a community."

"That, too."

"So it's all right that I'm here?" she asked even though she knew he would say yes no matter what.

"It's fantastic. And a surprise. I've been trying to figure out why since you called."

"Ah, that." She parted from him, took a look around. There was the big screen awkwardly hung half over very unique flowered wallpaper and half over the tallest wainscoting she'd ever seen. There was perhaps a foot of wallpaper showing, and the rest was green-and-white-striped wood with a small shelf thing running above the wainscoting across the length of the room. Here, too, were more comfy couches, two big recliners, more tables, but what really caught her interest were the photographs.

They were on every wall, on every tabletop. She started on the far wall over a console table. There was Jake as a kid, a little kid with a new bike complete with training wheels, smiling like he'd won the grandest prize of all. And there was his father, a young man standing proud in his NYPD uniform.

Her gaze stopped at an elegant picture of a woman with her dark hair in an updo, her makeup a little dated, but still tasteful, and Jake's eyes. That same blue, arresting, with dark, thick lashes Rebecca doubted were fake. She had a smile that was a little shy, but sweet, and there was a glow about her, as if she was looking at someone very special when the photographer had snapped the picture.

"She was a knockout," Jake said. "Oh, man, was my old man proud of her. He loved to take her dancing. There was a place in Park Slope that was an old-fashioned ballroom joint. No live orchestra, but they went there a lot. They were too young to be dancing like that, teased by all their friends, but they could dance. They won contests. Not a lot, nothing major. Didn't matter, that's not why they went."

"How long has she been gone?"

"Twelve years."

"I'm sorry."

Jake inhaled. "Me, too. She was a good mom. A little crazy. She liked to experiment with dinner. She sucked at that."

Rebecca laughed quietly as she put the picture back down. "Is there one of you in your uniform?"

He nodded, took her hand. They walked across the broad living room. It had the same hardwood flooring, but there was a big area rug in the center, deep green, which went with the wallpaper and the stripes. At the other end sat a bookcase, the lower shelves crammed with books. The upper two shelves had a few trinkets: a fancy candle, what looked like a music box, a set of those nesting dolls. And one large photograph in a silver frame of a much-younger Jake. His uniform was slightly different from his father's, but she couldn't have pinpointed how. The pride that came through in his posture and his eyes was identical.

"Oh, my," she said, "what is it about a man in uniform?"

"Depends on the man. I've known some butt-ugly cops."

She tugged him close. "Something tells me you had to fight them off with a stick wearing that NYPD blue."

"Hey, it wasn't the uniform."

"No." She looked at him squarely. "I'm sure it was your modesty."

"You're a riot."

She tilted her head toward the door. "If I'm not mistaken, dinner has arrived."

"I hope you like soy bacon and tofu and no tomato sauce."

"Ha."

The look he gave her made her worry that he wasn't kidding, but not for long. Not that he didn't try, but his eyes couldn't hide the smile that only teased his lips. Then he kissed her, slow and lush, until she forgot to be worried at all, and when he was through, he led her back to the Gang of Three.

THE PIZZA BOXES WERE EMPTY except for several discarded crusts courtesy of Liam, lying open on the coffee table in the living room. Jake's father was in his wheelchair, Liam and Pete were in the recliners and Rebecca sat on the couch next to Jake. They weren't pressed together, but they were close enough for their hands to brush. Every time that happened, a pulse of excitement surged through his body, particularly behind his fly. It wasn't critical—he wasn't seventeen any longer—but it made him hyperaware of her.

Even above the odor of pizza and pepperoni and garlic and onion, he had identified her scent. She wasn't one of those women who changed perfume as often as clothes, and for that he was grateful. This scent, something he couldn't name or even categorize, had made an impact. If he didn't see her for ten years, he'd still know it was her.

That was the good part. The bad part was that Mike had started telling stories. Embarrassing stories. Of Jake's childhood. Jake had given his father the glare of a lifetime, but no. Mike, the old bastard, was undaunted and unafraid. The first two had been uncomfortable, but they were kind of typical—peeing his pants at four, breaking an incredibly expensive vase at the police captain's house when Jake was seven. But this one…

"…he had one hell of a lisp," he father said, already

laughing. What's worse, Pete and Liam were laughing just as hard, and Rebecca, caught up in the moment, grinned at him as if it was all fun and games.

"Shut up, old man," Jake said. "It's not even funny."

"It's goddamn adorable, Jakey, so sit back and take it like a man."

Jake groaned, dropped his head in his hands. The only question was whether he should leave or stay. Staying meant utter humiliation. Running was cowardly, and he was still trying to impress the woman he wasn't supposed to be dating.

"So one day, my wife gets a call from his teacher. He's in second grade, mind you. Six." His dad had to pause for a minute to wipe his thumb under his eyes. "At first, see, my wife was worried. That his teacher was crying, she sounded so weird on the phone. But then, see, it turns out she was laughing."

"Oh, God," Liam said. "This kills me. Every fucking time." His eyes widened as he turned to Rebecca. "Excuse my language. I'm sorry."

"It's all right," she said. "I've heard the word before." Then she brushed Jake's hand as she leaned forward. "I've even said it a few times."

Liam nodded at her, then went back to staring at the storyteller, the father who had no concern whatsoever for his only child, the man who was single-handedly driving away any chance for a relationship with Rebecca.

"So she was laughing," his dad continued, "hard. Because my boy, my beautiful son, had been eaten alive by mosquitoes the night before. He was a mess, I gotta say, it wasn't pretty. But right in the middle of class, and remember this was a Catholic school and his teacher was a nun, so right in the middle, Jakey here stands up and yells, 'Thister, thethe methquito biteth are a pain in my ath.'" Mike had to stop and laugh for a while, and he wasn't alone. "So the sister says, 'What did you say?' and Jake just yells it again. The sister was calling my wife to tell her Jake had to go to the doctor because he had a pretty bad allergy, but damn, that story. It went all over the neighborhood like wildfire, and to this day, we can be walking down the block, and someone will yell out, 'Thethe methquito biteth are a pain in my ath!'"

Jake sighed, waiting for this hell to be over. Knowing that if he was really lucky, and he did get to see Rebecca again, she was going to bring up the lisp. No one could seem to help it.

Of course she laughed. Why wouldn't she? It was a riot. It wasn't his fault he hadn't had any front teeth. He was only in second grade, for God's sake, and weren't nuns supposed to be caring? Gentle? Twenty-nine years later, and he still kept hearing about the goddamn methquitoes.

Rebecca turned to Jake and held his face between her hands and kissed him, sitting right there on the living room couch. "It must have been awful," she said. "But so adorable I can't even..."

"Adorable. Just what a man wants to hear."

"You should want to," she said, keeping her voice low, as private as possible. "Because it's a wonderful thing. I'm so glad I came."

"Could have done without the show-and-tell."

She let him go, but didn't sit back. "That was the betht part."

Behind her, with laughter still lingering, Liam stood and started putting away the empty boxes. Rebecca noticed, then squeezed Jake's hand. "Walk me outside?"

"Walk you to 5th, you mean. Unless you want to call a cab from here."

"No, a walk would be good after all that pizza."

He stood back as she said her goodbyes, and he wasn't quite as bothered by the story being told. Of course, he'd get his revenge as soon as possible, but for tonight, it was fine. And wasn't she something as she spoke to his old man, touching his shoulder, getting personal. Jake didn't hear what she said, but he saw his father's face. Her visit made things more complicated, but that wasn't so horrible either. At least for now.

By the time he'd helped her on with her coat, Liam and Pete had helped Mike upstairs so Jake was able to leave comfortably. The two men would stick around until he got back. Now, though, he put on his own coat and went outside into the cold night.

They were quiet for a while, walking, her hand in his. It felt a little weird to have had such a domestic night when he'd never imagined her that way.

"I hope it wasn't too weird for you, me being there," she said.

"Interesting. Good interesting," he added, quickly. "I didn't expect..."

"I know. Me neither. I actually came here to ask you something."

"Okay."

"You know that dinner I've been bitching about?"

"Yep. Wednesday night, right?"

"Yes." She paused walking, faced him. "I wondered if you might like to come. As my date. But it's okay if you don't want to. It's black tie, and you know the kind of people who are going to be there, and it might turn out to be the most boring night of your life. Although my cousin Charlie and his girlfriend, Bree, will be there, and the food will be fantastic, but honestly, you don't have to say yes—"

"Yes," he said. "I'd love to come as your date."

"Really?"

Her wide dark eyes stared up at him with surprise, and he couldn't be sure but he thought she might be blushing.

"Really. It would be my honor. Where and when?"

She let out a big sigh, then grabbed the back of his neck and pulled him down into a kiss that should have waited for a much more private venue. He didn't mind.

9

Of all the skills Rebecca had learned from her parents, the ability to appear calm in virtually any circumstance was one of the most useful. It hadn't come easily, but over the years she'd found that she could separate her inner landscape from the outer facade. As she stood in the middle of the banquet room at the Four Seasons, those boundaries were being stretched to the limit.

It was early yet, with only staff in attendance, and the room buzzed with a controlled chaos. What had Rebecca sweating wasn't the catering or the orchestra or even the extravagant floral arrangements still being fussed with, but her own ability to let the people she'd hired do their jobs without her overseeing every last detail.

And Jake.

He hadn't arrived; it was two hours before anyone was expected. Dani was here, and the catering manager and one of the staff concierges and many, many hands to make sure every place setting was meticulous, that the food was superb in freshness, flavor and eye appeal. She had already checked into the room she'd booked for the night. If she had a lick of sense, she'd go upstairs immediately, lie down for at least twenty minutes, then begin her personal preparation. Dani was also going to use the room to change clothes so Rebecca's window of opportunity for a short nap was closing.

"Go. Everything's fine," Dani said, which illustrated perfectly the need for her to get the hell out of there.

Rebecca glanced around, still hesitating.

Dani, dressed in black pants, a striped shirt and low heels, crossed her arms over her chest. "You're making everyone nuts. If anything's going to crash and burn it'll be because we're all trying to impress you."

"Oh." Rebecca gave it a minute's thought and could see the point. "Fine. I'll rest. But I'm going to have my cell in my hand so call me if anything happens. I mean anything."

Dani's only response was to cross her heart, then stare pointedly at the door.

Rebecca took her leave and while she was certain she'd be unable to think of a thing besides the enormous checklist for the dinner, once she stepped into the elevator, it was Jake. All Jake.

She hadn't asked him about his tux, because that would have been unbearably awful, but she'd worried about it. Then she'd worried about worrying. He was altogether a difficult issue for her. Ever since her conversation with Bree and Charlie, Rebecca had played over every motive, every wish, every daydream she'd had in the short time she'd known Jake. Since she'd visited his home, her confusion had worsened. Yet hearing his voice instantly stifled her qualms, making it crystal clear how much she liked him. All the same, an hour later she was chock-full of self-doubt and second-guessing.

She entered the lovely deluxe hotel room. She was planning to spend the night there even though she lived quite close to the hotel, but she wasn't sure if Jake would stay. She hoped so now, but she might not later. A lot depended on the success of the evening, particularly her success with William West. When she'd met with him at the Gates Foundation dinner, he'd seemed interested, although she wasn't sure if his interest was in the Winslow Foundation or her.

He hadn't been overt, not at all, but the signs had all been there. Lingering eye contact, a kiss to the back of her hand that had made her uncomfortable. It was very likely that he was behaving the way he behaved with all women. He wouldn't be the first man she'd met who was like that. Under other circumstances, she wouldn't bother finding out the truth, but he had a substantial fortune he wanted to donate, and she was only one among many in line for it.

She just hoped she'd have a definitive read on him by the end of the evening. The last thing she wanted to do was waste time playing games.

She settled on the bed, her cell phone clutched in her right hand. She closed her eyes, but didn't expect to sleep. There would be dancing. The orchestra was fantastic, and they weren't going to go crazy with too modern a set because there wasn't a person attending who would know what to do to hip-hop. Well, maybe Bree and Charlie, but still. There would be slow numbers, mostly, and medium numbers, but nothing that would make anyone sweaty.

She had no idea how much of that, if any, Jake's leg could take. She'd prefer not to put him in an uncomfortable situation but that was unavoidable, wasn't it? And why was she even worried in the first place? If he had thought it was a bad idea, he'd have declined the invitation. He wasn't a child and he had nothing to prove to her.

God, they weren't even dating. Although they might as well be because there were going to be a hell of a lot of Winslows in The Cosmopolitan Suite. Her parents, to begin with. Her grandfather. Charlie. Andrew, her cousin on her mother's side, who was not terribly bright. He did, however, look great in photographs which was evidently all the family thought he needed to run for the New York senate. He'd be pressing the flesh, distracting and irritating everyone and taking the spotlight off the foundation.

She wouldn't think about that because there was nothing she could do about it. The Winslow family had her outvoted, and if she was honest with herself, she'd known keeping Andrew away was a lost cause before the discussion had come up.

She hated it, though. He was a jerk, and New York deserved so much better.

She moaned as she turned over. The nap was a farce, but maybe a shower would soothe her enough to deal with the rest of her night. She thought about asking her mother to bring one of her nice little calming pills with her, but rejected the notion immediately. If ever she needed to be sharp it was tonight.

She got her things together for her shower, made sure her dress and shoes were at the ready, then went into the bathroom, purposely leaving her cell phone on the bedside table.

JAKE ENTERED THE FOUR SEASONS from the East 57th Street entrance and walked into the elevator that would take him down one level to The Cosmopolitan Suite, unashamed to admit that he was nervous. He knew how to behave with high-end company, that wasn't it. He wanted to impress Rebecca. At the very least, he wanted to be what she needed, although it didn't help that he wasn't sure what that would be.

First thing, he'd find himself a drink. Okay, second thing, because as he entered the banquet room, there she was. And she was a stunner.

Man, she looked like a movie star. Like a forties glamour girl, and he had to wonder if her choice in gowns had anything to do with their recent discussions of film noir. No, that was a ridiculous thought especially when he took into account that the style fit her to a T.

The dress was floor-length, a rich red that showed off her creamy shoulders and amazing curves. Her hair was pinned up, her lips red, and when she caught sight of him, there was nothing and no one else in the room. The smile that lit up her face got him moving. By the time he reached her, she had turned, and while he wanted to kiss her until the sun came up tomorrow, he stopped himself in the nick of time. Instead he followed her lead. She took one hand and squeezed it and kissed his cheek, then whispered, "I'm so glad you're here."

He nodded slightly, then forced himself to cool it as he realized they were most definitely not alone. Not five feet away, Jake recognized a guy who had his arm around a really petite, pretty girl. On further inspection, she wasn't that young. Just small. And decked out in a dress that made him blink. Not that she didn't look great in it, she did. It was just odd with pastel colors in a weirdly geometric jacket on top of a black-and-white-striped skirt and shoes that seemed to be made solely of straps.

"Jake Donnelly, this is my cousin Charlie Winslow, and my friend Bree Kingston. They'll be sitting with you when I'm roaming around shaking hands, so it would be better if you liked each other."

"Sure, no pressure," Jake said, as he shook hands with first Bree, then Charlie. "You're the blog guy. I don't know why I didn't make the connection."

"I am the blog guy, but in this room, I'm just Rebecca's cousin," Charlie said. "Nice to meet you."

Bree said, "You know what? I could use a drink. How about you boys go fetch us some?"

"It's all equality until someone needs a drink or there's a spider in the bathtub," Charlie said. "You want pineapple juice or something for grown-ups?"

Bree gave Charlie a quick glare. "A Sea Breeze, please."

Jake turned to Rebecca. "And you?"

"I don't dare start drinking this early. I'll have a tonic and lime. That'll fool everyone, right?"

"No one's going to notice. They'll all be too dazzled by how beautiful you are."

"Oh," Bree said as if she'd just seen a kitten. "Okay, you can stay."

He laughed to hide the embarrassment of having been such a cliché, but the look on Rebecca's face told him he hadn't crossed the unforgivable line. "Be right back."

He and Charlie went toward the nearest bar and Jake finally took a look at the joint. It was huge; there was a stage with a full orchestra playing something soft and jazzy, enormous vases with huge flower arrangements all around the many tables, each set up with more glittering silver and crystal than he'd seen in Macy's. It was a massive affair, this party, and he slowed his pace as he watched a row of servers enter the ballroom. They were in black and white, wore gloves and held silver platters with tiny hors d'oeuvres on them. Jesus. She'd said there were billions at stake but he only believed her now. She was playing in the majors.

"You used to be a cop?" Charlie asked as they reached the bar.

"Yeah. Got in right after college. Planned on staying until retirement. Didn't work out that way."

Since there wasn't much of a line yet, they were able to order pretty quickly. Charlie went first, then Jake put in his requests. He glanced back to find Bree and Rebecca huddled, both staring directly at him. Great.

"Don't worry," Charlie said. "You already passed. Rebecca wouldn't have invited you if you were even marginal. Tonight is huge for her. It's like the Super Bowl of fundraisers."

"She's amazing."

"That she is," Charlie said. "The only relative I like, which is something because we've got relatives crawling out of the woodwork. I'll do my best to help you avoid as many as possible."

"She told me her folks would be here."

"Her father isn't a Winslow by birth, but he might as well have been. He's got the entitlement thing down to a science." Charlie got his drinks and waited for Jake. "We all do, honestly. We grew up on the milk of privilege, but Rebecca has always handled it like a responsibility, not a game. She could have done anything with her life. The foundation used to be more of a tax dodge than a charitable enterprise, but she's changing all that. It's not easy, considering who's on the board."

It was Jake's turn to get his drinks, and he took advantage of the moment to take a good sip of his bourbon and water. Although he'd have to grab some of those appetizers before long. He wasn't about to get drunk, not tonight. "We haven't talked all that much about our respective careers," he said. "Although I checked out the foundation online. Seems to be doing a lot of good work."

Charlie brought them to the women, drinks were exchanged, but he didn't stop looking at Jake. "You can tell me to go jump in a lake," Charlie said, "but I've gotta ask the guy question. You got shot? Twice?"

Jake had been expecting that since he and Rebecca had met, but not from her cousin. It didn't bother him. Charlie was right. Every guy he knew had hit him up for details. He wondered though if it had been a setup. If Rebecca had wanted to know and asked Charlie to front the question. From the look on her face, he didn't think that was the case. She probably did want to know so he plunged ahead.

"Undercover operation. Didn't go so well. We trusted someone who didn't deserve it. There was a shoot-out like you see on cop shows on TV. I'd never seen anything like it before, and I didn't see it for long.

"I was lucky, I would have bled out if there hadn't been paramedics right there. The getting shot part wasn't at all like on TV. It hurt like a sonofabitch, and it didn't heal up by the next commercial. I still go to rehab, my left hand shakes from time to time and I'll be living with this limp for the rest of my life."

Charlie held up his drink. "Thank you for your service. I'm sorry it cost such a high price."

Rebecca had lost her smile, but she held her drink up in salute, as did Bree.

Jake wasn't good at this, and did what he always did, which was to look at his shoes. "Thanks." When he looked up again, it was at Rebecca. "How about them Yankees?"

REBECCA IGNORED BREE AND Charlie completely. She kissed Jake on the lips. "I have to do things. I'll come back. I promise."

"Go," Jake said. "Knock 'em dead. As if you could help it."

A little "oh" let her know Bree had been listening, but Rebecca continued to ignore her friend. "I wish I didn't have to go. But duty calls." She pasted on a smile, went toward the entrance and began the fundraising portion of the evening.

While she welcomed guests that never failed to appear in *Time* magazine's 100 Most Influential People, some of them her own relatives, she couldn't resist sneaking glances back at Jake.

She wasn't sure of the designer of his tux, for all she knew it could be off the rack, but it didn't matter because the man wore the clothes, not the other way around. Did he ever.

It was traditional black, complete with bow tie and small pocket kerchief, white. The classic look was a fantastic frame for his face, his *eyes,* and she dared any woman in the room not to swoon over him after one sight.

"Rebecca." The strident voice couldn't be mistaken for any other.

Rebecca returned to her duties. "Hello, Mom. Dad." She bent for the air kisses and waited for the verdict. Both parents would have something to say about her, about the room, about the night, about every last little detail right down to the type of gloves worn by the waitstaff.

"You look very nice," her mother said. "Although you may want to rethink the strapless gowns when it comes to this particular event. You represent the entire family, and we wouldn't want anyone getting the wrong idea."

"I'm pretty certain everyone here would be able to tell I was a woman even if I wore a burka, Mother. And how's your hip, Dad? Better?"

Her father ignored the question. "The Bannerman Orchestra?" He sighed. It was all he needed to do.

"I like the way they rock the Hokey Pokey. Go get yourselves drinks. Have a good time. I made sure to have your favorite caviar to go with the Cristal Champagne. And don't annoy Charlie. He's in a mood."

Neither of them deigned to reply as they walked over to the bar. Rebecca had to admit they looked fantastic, but then the Winslows and the Thorpes had learned the art of presentation when they were toddlers.

And then she caught sight of Jake and he was looking at her, ignoring his companions, as far as she could tell. She smiled. He smiled back. When she held out her hand to Mr. and Mrs. Chandler, she knew she was blushing.

Time slipped by in a mixture of false bonhomie and genuine pleasure as she continued to schmooze the elite. The orchestra played old standards, reserving those best for dancing until later. Soon dinner would be served and while she couldn't wait for the seating, which would only come after she'd made her welcome speech, she was becoming concerned since William West hadn't arrived yet.

She'd felt sure he'd have come early, ready to continue the flirting he'd started last Thursday night. Well, she wouldn't really worry until halfway through dinner.

IT WASN'T A BIG SURPRISE that Charlie was great. He was Rebecca's favorite cousin, and made it to the list of things they both liked. So far he'd added good vodka, pizza crusts, his salad-making expertise, a deep appreciation for her underwear, film noir and the kind of sex that could start wars. Bree was cool, too. She made him laugh, and he appreciated the way she was with Charlie. Easy, but connected. They hadn't been together long, but he'd wager the relationship would take.

His folks used to look at each other like these two did. As if the words were nice, but unnecessary.

Rebecca's voice on the stage snapped his gaze back to her. Dammit, the woman knocked him out. Not just the way she was gorgeous, but the way she held the attention of every person in the room. Yeah, he wasn't such a Brooklyn yahoo that he didn't recognize half the people in attendance. Christ, he read the papers. Watched the news. What the hell he was doing here, he had no idea.

That question was becoming something of a problem. Anyone with half a brain would know he and Rebecca were a temporary item. There was zero chance that he was anything more than a passing whim. The issue was that he was starting to care about that. About after.

Who was going to measure up to a woman like Rebecca Thorpe? It wasn't about the money thing, the hell with the money. But the woman? The heat between them? How he felt when he was with her? Yeah, who would he ever meet that would begin to compare?

The crowd laughed at something Rebecca had said and he found her looking at him instead of her audience. For a minute, she lost the gleam in her eye, and that was all on him. He hadn't been paying attention, and, dammit, that was his job, his only job. To support her. To make her feel like a million. Well, in this group, a billion. He smiled and hoped like hell he could put her back on track.

The next words out of her mouth were confident,

smooth. Amusing. She was back, and he wasn't going to think about the unknowable future. He was here, now, and he'd be a moron not to enjoy every last second.

10

REBECCA BARELY TOUCHED her sole meunìere. Pity, because the food was unbelievably wonderful. She hated that her plate would go to waste.

If she could have she would have scooted her chair closer to Jake's until she could lean against him. She wanted his arm around her shoulders, his soft kiss in her hair. Instead, she contented herself with watching him enjoy his beef tenderloin, the sound of his laughter when Charlie or Bree said something amusing. It puzzled her, how much she enjoyed merely looking at him. At the funny and incredibly endearing way he would express himself with a quirk of his lips. He could transform from the essence of machismo to the picture of infinite kindness when he saw his father's hands.

She put another small bite into her mouth when Bree caught her eye. She pointedly glanced at Jake, then bit her lower lip as if Jake's pure awesomeness was too much to handle. Rebecca laughed, covering her mouth, trying not to choke.

"You okay?" Jake asked, his hand on her bare back above her dress.

She hissed at the contact even though his hand wasn't cold or a surprise.

He lifted it immediately at the sound, but she shook her head. "No, it's fine. I'm fine."

Jake was pulling away when her hand found his thigh. "It felt good," she said.

His smile unfolded slowly in all its slightly crooked glory as he touched her again. He kept his voice low, and she felt his breath on the shell of her ear. "You've nailed this," he said. "Listen. You can hear that people are enjoying themselves. I couldn't swear to it, but I bet for this crowd, that's unusual. Your fingerprints are all over this night. You should hit them hard as soon as the meal is over. They're pumped and primed."

She laughed again, but it was breathless at his compliments. She did as he'd suggested. She listened. The orchestra was on a break as she'd specified no music during dinner. She wanted people to talk. Above the clatter of silver, the clink of glasses, there was a steady mumble of voices, nothing distinct but the laughter.

She looked over her left shoulder to the nearest table. Not one of the guests was staring blankly while they ate. Everyone was engaged, participating. It was only one table, but indicative.

Her attention shifted to her immediate surroundings. Wine was being poured. Jake's hand rubbed a small circle on her back and her stomach tightened. Charlie asked Bree if she liked the amaranth; Bree told him she wasn't sure because she had no idea what amaranth was.

She hardly realized she had turned to face Jake, that she'd found his gaze and was staring, watching his pupils grow as his breathing quickened. "Thank you," she said. Then she kissed him on the lips. It was tempting to stay there, with his hand on her back and his words swimming in her head. But that would have to wait.

When she sat up, he drew away smoothly. He took up his fork and had another bite of the eggplant puree. His amaranth remained untouched. Perhaps it would have been wiser to go with a rice pilaf.

Rebecca was sidetracked by movement at the front door. William West had finally arrived. Although she couldn't make out the details, how he ripped off his coat told her everything about his mood. So much for getting him to commit to an endowment tonight.

Then again, maybe not. Once he'd turned back from getting his coat checked, all signs of tension had vanished and he appeared to be his usual confident self as his gaze swept the room. He found her quickly, giving her a courtly nod.

He wasn't much to look at. Average height, brown hair, a body that spoke of a golf hobby instead of a gym membership. He counted on his net worth to give him sex appeal.

Dani met him at the door, but West turned his back on her, which made Rebecca sit up damn straight. A woman Rebecca didn't recognize then entered, wearing what looked like a very politically incorrect full-length fur. She was tall and slim and beautiful, and she looked good as she smiled at Mr. West. She also looked very young, but that was par for the course in this crowd.

Interesting that while West had sent his RSVP in for two, he'd led her to believe that his CFO was going to join him. Well, perhaps the leggy brunette was the CFO.

West took the woman's arm and Dani led them to their table, making sure the waiter was on her heels with both wine and champagne.

Dani went from there directly to the kitchen. Rebecca

relaxed, knowing the next course would be delayed in order to give West and his guest time to catch up. Luckily, the fourth course was salad, and when it did arrive, the removal of plates would be handled perfectly. She may have begrudged spending the money on this particular ballroom, but the catering staff at the Four Seasons was impeccable, always.

For the first time that night, she lifted her wineglass. Part two of fundraising: the hard sell, would come all too soon, but she could handle it. Jake said so.

JAKE HAD LOST BOTH BREE and Charlie. Him to the bar in search of pineapple juice, and Bree to the ladies' room. Jake had watched in amazement as the banquet tables had been replaced by a dance floor and a number of cocktail tables had been set up on the periphery of the room. The entire operation hadn't taken ten minutes. Impressive.

He'd found a spot far enough away from the dancing to avoid being stepped on while leaving the tables for the more needful among the crowd. He normally didn't mind standing; he just wasn't sure how his leg was going to hold out.

A hand on his arm had him turning, expecting Bree. It was, in fact, a woman he'd noticed earlier. He'd place her age in her late fifties, mostly because of the obvious work she'd had done. He doubted very much lips that large had come direct from the factory, or that she'd been born looking so surprised. What had struck him before was that, according to the papers, she and her husband owned a large portion of Manhattan, so obviously the woman could have afforded the best in plastic surgeons. Hell, maybe she was actually in her eighties and the doctors had outdone themselves.

"I don't know you," she said, her words slurred with whiskey. He imagined she wore a very nice perfume, but it couldn't compete with the booze. "But you know Rebecca. Very well, I'm thinking."

"I'm glad to say she's a friend," he replied, smiling as pleasantly as he could.

"Friend, my ass. I'm Paulina."

"Nice to meet you," he said, holding out his hand. "Jake."

"You're the best-looking thing at this dinner. Did you know that?"

He bit back a laugh. "That's very kind of you."

"Oh, don't get excited," she said, waving her hand so that her jewels flashed against the lights. "I'm not going to do anything about it. My husband doesn't even mind. He knows I like to look."

"Paulina!"

Jake looked up at Charlie's voice, more grateful than he could say.

"We haven't seen each other in ages," Charlie said, taking her hand and spinning her away from Jake. "You get more beautiful every time I see you." He gave her two air kisses and a smile that looked one hundred percent real.

"Charlie. Honey. You're the best-looking thing at this dinner. Did you know that?"

"I did, Paulina, I did. There doesn't seem to be a damn thing I can do about it, though. I'm just that handsome."

She waved her hand again, laughing, and Charlie shoved a glass of juice at Jake before he guided the woman into the crowd.

"So he's thrown me over for another woman," Bree said, making Jake jump. The damn orchestra made it hard to know when people were approaching. "Is that my drink?"

He handed her the glass, then took a sip from his own. "He rescued me. Don't give him any grief."

"Well, damn, there goes my night."

"You're good together, you two."

She grinned happily. "I think so. It's weird though."

"What?"

"Him being Charlie Winslow. I'm from Ohio. Before I moved in with Charlie, I shared a tiny one-bedroom apartment with four people. Now we share a floor. A whole floor."

"It is kind of overwhelming," he said. "How really rich they are. But most of the time, I don't think about it."

"I ignored it when Charlie and I first started going out, but it's too big to ignore. It takes adjusting, on both our parts. He doesn't even get it half the time. What he has access to is insane. His normal is about fifty times grander than my wildest fantasies."

Jake thought about Rebecca's condo; the view alone let him know he was in over his head. "I don't think I'll be around long enough to have to adjust."

"Oh, no." Bree stepped in front of him, pouting. It was actually very cute. "Don't say that. Why did you say that? You guys are so great together."

"We're not even dating. Not for real. I have no idea why I'm here. We were a kind of setup thing. A mutual acquaintance. In theory, it was for one night only."

"Huh," Bree said, trying to hide her grin. "That's a familiar tale."

"Oh?"

"*Our* mutual acquaintance was Rebecca."

"Huh," he repeated.

Bree just wiggled her eyebrows.

Behind Bree, he caught sight of Rebecca, and the urge to join her was strong despite the fact that he knew she was working the room. She'd told him as much, apologetically, which he appreciated, but leaving no room for misinterpretation. Tonight was business, and he was… not.

On the other hand, her glass was empty. She kept bringing it up to her lips to drink, then lowering it as she recalled the tonic was gone.

"Charlie's on his way back," he said to Bree. "So if you'll excuse me."

"Sure," she said, glancing from him to Rebecca then back. "Go get her, tiger."

He ignored the crazy girl and went toward the bar. It took him longer than he'd like to get Rebecca's drink, but when he found her again, she was still talking to the same guy, and her glass was still empty. Jake's approach was stealthy, not wanting to disrupt the flow of her conversation, yet keeping the man's back to him so that Rebecca had a little warning.

Only, when he got close enough, he heard the guy laugh. The sound stopped Jake short. He'd heard that laugh before. One other time, twelve years ago. He'd never forgotten it, not a chance, because it had belonged to Vance Keegan.

"Lip" Keegan had been part of a very large drug bust. He'd escaped, along with about half a dozen others, when things had gone to hell. Unlike the other runners, Keegan had seemed to vanish into thin air.

Jake moved in slowly, trying to avoid Rebecca's attention until he could convince himself that he'd been mistaken. Even though the laugh was a dead ringer for Bender, a *Futurama* cartoon character, there had to be more than one person who sounded like that. Jake had been in charge of getting Keegan into the bus. He'd cuffed the guy, had him by the arm, and he'd let him get away. The piece of crap had laughed the whole way across the rooftop, a full block, right in Jake's ear. But that had happened a lifetime ago, when Jake had been a rookie.

The man with the uncanny laugh stepped closer to Rebecca. He reached over and touched her above the elbow. Jake moved in, right up between them, no excuses. Keegan stepped back, which was the point. Except it wasn't Keegan.

The face wasn't the same. The eyes were different, the shape of his jaw, his nose had been bigger. But shit, shit, under the mustache, this guy had been born with a cleft pallet. Same as Lip Keegan.

"Jake," Rebecca said. "Is everything all right?"

He forced himself to look at Rebecca. As soon as he did, the time and place came back to him with a jolt. He must have made a mistake, which was weird and embarrassing enough, but he'd intruded on what could have been a crucial moment. "I apologize. I lost my footing," he said, even more embarrassed that he was using his injuries to excuse himself. "I meant to refresh your drink."

His lame excuse, God, the pun made him wince, had done its job. Rebecca visibly relaxed and her smile wasn't at all forced.

"I'll leave you to it," he said, trading glasses with her.

"Wait," she said, touching his arm. "I'd like you to meet William West. The CEO of West Industries."

"Bill," he said. Dammit, that wasn't the same scar. Lip's scar had been jagged, a mess. "You are?"

Jake took the offered hand. "Jake Donnelly. A friend of Rebecca's." The handshake was tight, and Jake supposed he was fifty percent responsible, but all his instincts were telling him that West was not who he claimed to be. Jake thought about Paulina and her artificial face, and he wondered. With someone good on the end of a scalpel, it was possible.

"Thanks for the drink," Rebecca said, startling him again.

"My pleasure. I'll see you later." He nodded at West, then left, achingly aware of his limp and his confusion. He knew nothing about West Industries, but he did know that Keegan would have had twelve years to change his face, to reinvent himself.

On the other hand, the likelihood of Jake running into Vance Keegan at the Four Seasons was absurd. Still, he'd check it out, because even if the odds were he was as wrong as he could get, West was involved with Rebecca. If West did end up giving a grant or donation or whatever the hell people gave to foundations, Jake needed to be sure it wasn't blood money. Rebecca would never want that.

She would want him here. Thinking about her, instead of a long-shot hunch.

He ordered a bourbon at the bar, left a tip, then went straight back to Charlie and Bree, still standing near the dance floor. Charlie had his arms wrapped around her and they looked completely into each other. In love. Jake put aside his concerns and played his part as if his life depended on it.

THE ORCHESTRA CAME BACK from their break as Bill West kissed the back of Rebecca's hand. The gesture was creepy, but then the man was creepy, so what could she expect? It didn't matter whether she liked him or not, or that he'd flirted with her right in front of his girlfriend, companion, whatever she was. It wasn't difficult to see his *friend* hadn't been too thrilled. Rebecca wasn't either—not about the flirting, but how they'd ended the conversation. Even though West had said he was going to get involved with the foundation, no promise had been made, no dollar amount mentioned, and she'd needed both of those to happen tonight. On the plus side, they were going to meet privately later in the week. On the minus side, she'd have to see him privately.

Now the only pressing matter was finding Jake. She hadn't yet introduced him to her parents, and while that prospect wasn't thrilling, she figured she'd better. The last thing she'd want was for Jake to think she'd kept them apart. He'd never believe it was because she didn't want him to meet them, not the other way around.

She missed Jake, even though he was in the same room. She liked him. He'd brought her a tonic and lime because he'd noticed her glass was empty. Didn't sound like much, but in her experience it was almost unprecedented.

She spotted him on the other side of the dance floor. He'd been watching her. People kept blocking her line of sight, but only for seconds at a time as they danced by. He stayed where he was, watching, waiting. The room filled with the sound of strings, the violins romantic and dazzling, the cellos low and sexy.

They had to walk around the dance floor, but eventually, Jake was in front of her. She could reach out and touch him if she wanted.

She wanted.

Her hand went to the back of his neck and she drew him into a kiss. For a long moment there was nothing but his lips, the slide of his tongue, the warmth that spread through her body. He broke away, not far. She could still feel his breath on her chin.

"I'd sure like to do more of that," he said.

"Me, too. Will you stay the night? I have a room upstairs."

"Of course I will."

She brushed the back of his hand with hers. She wanted to steal him away, forget the party, the introductions, the good-nights.

"I know you have to go back to your duties," he said. "Dance with me first? Fair warning, it's not going to be pretty."

"Pretty is overrated."

They put their drinks on the nearest table and went to a corner of the dance floor, where Jake took her around her waist, drawing her close. Rebecca slipped her arms around his neck, rested her head on his shoulder. They didn't so much dance as sway, and even that was bumpy because Jake had to make adjustments.

It was altogether perfect.

The rest of the night would be so much more bearable knowing Jake would be there at the end.

11

At one in the morning, there was absolutely nothing Jake wanted more than to get out of the ballroom, out of his tuxedo and into Rebecca. It didn't look like an escape was imminent, though.

He'd have figured the orchestra would have stopped playing by midnight, but nope. They kept on pumping out tunes, most of them a little peppier than the sleepy waltzes they'd featured when the crowd had been at its peak. Charlie and Bree had cut out over an hour ago, and William West had left an hour before them. Unfortunately, Rebecca was still being set upon by people who clearly didn't have work tomorrow. For God's sake, it was a Wednesday night.

Rebecca continued to look stunning. As if she'd just arrived. Not a hair out of place, her dress as beautiful and slinky as it had been when he'd first seen her. How did women do it? Stand up all night on tiptoe? High heels had to hurt like a sonofabitch.

He went over to the buffet table where they'd put out coffee and pastries a while ago. Since his leg was as tired as the rest of him, he was fingering one of his pain pills in his tux pocket. It didn't normally knock him out, but he didn't normally drink when he took the pill.

The coffee turned out to be a good idea. Sipping something hot and familiar made him feel more relaxed, let him give his obsessive mind a rest.

If he wasn't thinking about Rebecca, he was thinking about West. Keegan. That damn laugh, the lip. It was driving him crazy. That's what happened to a man when there wasn't a problem to solve that was more difficult than how to install bathroom tile. The mind turned to mush.

He was sinking into a really good sulk when he saw Rebecca coming toward him. He straightened, not giving a damn about his leg now, or his need for sleep. The nearer she got, the better his mood. Until he realized why the couple behind her looked so familiar. She'd said she was going to introduce him to her parents.

Fuck.

He put his coffee down on the buffet table and surreptitiously wiped his right hand on his slacks. Rebecca's smile would have put him at ease if her parents hadn't been right behind her.

"I'm sorry it's so late," she said, placing her hand on his arm and moving to his side. "I did want to introduce you to my parents before we left for the evening. Marjorie and Franklin, this is Jake Donnelly."

He shook their hands. He smiled, but only slightly, kept his cool because he had been trained by the best captain in the continental United States, and he did not give away the game under any kind of pressure. "Pleasure to meet you both."

"Rebecca hasn't told us much about you, Jake. What is it that you do?" Franklin's nonsmile reminded Jake of politicians and backstreet lawyers. He was unnaturally tan for March in New York, and he was fighting lean.

His wife was a beauty, and Rebecca favored her. Same honey-blond hair, same long face that sat right on the border of attractive in Marjorie's case.

"I'm unemployed at the moment," he said. "Doing some work on my father's house. Figuring out what comes next."

"Unemployed?" Franklin said.

"Yes, sir." Jake had been shot in the line of duty. He was under no obligation to explain himself. A glance at Rebecca told him she'd have no problem if he left it at that. But these were her folks. He didn't need to prove anything by being a dick, either. "I was in the NYPD. Major Case Squad detective. I was injured in the line of duty and took early retirement. I haven't decided yet where I'll land when I've healed up."

Franklin stopped looking at Jake as if he was infectious.

"That must have been terrible for you," Rebecca's mother said.

"It hasn't been a picnic, but I'm still here."

"And we're still *here,*" Rebecca said, leaving his side to kiss her father on the cheek, then her mother. "It's late. Go home. I'm going to sleep soon."

"Tonight was very well done," Marjorie said.

"Thanks, Mom."

Franklin said nothing. He nodded, then took his wife's arm and went for the coat check.

Rebecca turned back to Jake. "Thank you. I probably should have prepared them."

"For what? That I'm so good-looking?"

She grinned. "That, too. They mean well. They're dinosaurs, you know? Stuck in time with very rigid boundaries. Charlie's parents, too. The whole family, actually. I think they stopped evolving when they got lucky during the thirties."

"Speaking of which," he said, sliding his hands around her waist. "That dress makes me think of smoky jazz clubs and men in fedoras."

"You'd look great in a hat."

"I have a hat."

"Really?"

"I'll wear it for you sometime."

"Do me a favor?" she asked.

"Whatever you want."

"Don't wear anything else when you show me."

He kissed her. Nothing too extravagant, not yet. Merely a preview of coming attractions.

Later, despite his best intentions and Rebecca's outstanding choice in underwear, she was so obviously exhausted when they finally climbed into the big hotel bed at two-twenty, that he couldn't do anything but hold her as she fell asleep.

By all rights, he should have been out like a light himself, but maybe it was the coffee, maybe how far out of his comfort zone he'd been all night, but he stared at the sliver of light coming in from the privacy drapes as his thoughts bounced around like a nine-ball off three rails.

If it wasn't about how much he wanted to see Rebecca again, it was about how stupid he was for wanting to see Rebecca again, and if neither of those made his gut tighten enough, he settled on the odds of William West being Vance Keegan 2.0, hiding his corrupt past with a fake identity and some excellent plastic surgery.

It took him a hell of a long time to get to sleep, but at least Rebecca was using his good shoulder for a pillow. That made up for a lot.

WAKING UP TO NO ALARM AND Jake wrapped around her like a warm blanket was everything a girl could want out of life. He must not have been up for too long if his fuzzy smile was anything to go by.

"Morning," she said, careful not to breathe in his direction.

He kissed her forehead. "Morning, gorgeous. I'm thinking about ordering up a lot of coffee. Maybe some French toast. You like French toast?"

She nodded, stifling a yawn. "I'll go do stuff," she said. "But save my shower for after."

"That's a hell of an idea."

"There are robes. In the bathroom. Big, thick white robes. I'll bring you one."

"Thanks. Anything else you want from room service?"

She shook her head, then felt him watch her ass as she walked away.

They lingered over food, teasing each other with cool feet sneaking up naked legs. Jake, aside from looking at her as if she was stunning despite her raccoon eyes and hair from her nightmares, continued to be amazing. Crazy amazing, like someone had built him to her exact specifications.

He did a recap of the evening that made her laugh and blush, showering her with kudos. Nothing would have pleased her more than spending the rest of the day in bed. And the night. Unfortunately, she did have to leave by two because as much as she deserved a day off, she wasn't going to get one. There were too many details to handle, her own notes and follow-up calls to enter on her calendar.

But it was only noon now. She put her cup down, then took his cup and put it on the room service tray. The edges of his lips curled up as she untied the robe's belt and pushed the thick terry cloth off his shoulders. She could only get so far, but Jake was quick, and he took over where she left off. She stripped herself bare, then rested once again on her knees.

Naked and mostly hard, Jake reached for her, cupping her cheek in his large hand. "You take my breath away," he said. "I want you all the time."

She turned her head to kiss his thumb. "Make love to me?"

"Yes." He shifted his hands to her shoulders and eased them both down on the bed until they were on their sides, inches apart, their gazes holding. "I never know where to start with you. If I go for the kiss, I can't see the rest of you. I don't have enough hands to touch every part of your body at once. I love being inside you, and believe me, I'm a big fan of coming, but then I have to rest, and that seems like such a waste."

It wasn't the same giddy shiver in her tummy. As strong, yes, but not the same. This was a warmth, deep down, that spread into her limbs and her chest and her throat and her hands. They met in a kiss, and he tasted like Jake beneath the maple and coffee.

As his hand ran down her arm, slowly, gently, tears built behind her closed lids. She liked him so much, she didn't know what to do with it. This was new. A part of herself hidden all these years. Triggered by his touch and how he saw her. So calm, so assured. He didn't care about her lineage or that she could be a snob or that she lived in a bubble of privilege. He had looked past all of it from that first night.

What surprised her even more was that she didn't care that he had no job, that his body was torn up, that he lived in a world she'd barely known existed.

His kiss deepened and she was on her back, with Jake settling between her legs. Everything felt slow as honey; even the light coming in from the terrace window steeped them in amber. She touched him, ran her palms down his back and over his shoulders and felt the muscles move beneath his skin. She breathed his breath and they rubbed against each other in a slow, easy dance that could have gone on forever. There was no rush to get to the finish line. This was enough. This was heaven.

She looked at his dark hair, mussed from sleep and her fingers, then down his strong back, so beautiful. Even the scar was a map of his character. He'd survived so much. He should have been bitter. Mad at the world. But that wasn't Jake.

He was a wonder. He'd expanded her world. He made her laugh and made her come and he was a terrible dancer. The way he talked to his father was something she'd dreamed of as a child. That she would wake up one day and her family would be close and they'd laugh together at silly things. That her dad would light up when she walked into a room. It was all so tempting.

Yet as much as Jake filled her with joy, she couldn't picture a future with him. But she wanted to. God, she wanted to.

She loved him. Oh, what had she done?

"You're trembling," he said.

Her fingers had gripped him so tightly, she had to be hurting him. She spread her thighs, lifted her hips with an urgency that hadn't been there a few moments ago. "Make love to me. Please."

He looked at her, his lips moist from her kisses, his eyes curious and a little worried. "Yes," he said again.

When he stretched to reach the condoms left on the bedside table, she clung to him even as she loosened her grip.

JAKE GOT HOME AT four-thirty that afternoon, still tired, leg and shoulder aching. The boys were on the porch, of course, giving him hell.

"My goodness, that was some party," Pete said, leaning back in his plastic chair. "I didn't think those fancy dress shindigs lasted all night."

"Maybe now he's been with hoi polloi," Liam added, "he doesn't want to hang out with us regular Joes."

Jake made it up the porch stairs and shook his head at the old busybodies. "Hoi polloi doesn't mean what you think it means," he said.

"Oh, so now we don't know English." Liam shifted. "Well, excuse me."

"I'm tired and cold and I need to get out of this damn monkey suit. But feel free to make fun of me in absentia."

The old men laughed, poking at each other as Jake hit the door. He gave his dad a grin, then went inside. Shower first, then he'd hit the computer. The downstairs unfinished bathroom made him groan with guilt. He'd get to it, but first, he had to see if there was any current record of Vance Keegan. Maybe the guy was in prison, maybe, more likely, he was long dead.

After another set of stairs, each step harder to climb, Jake started a hot bath, then went back to his room to put on some normal clothes. It wasn't as if he'd hated the party or felt overly uncomfortable. He just couldn't see making a habit of it.

That was the fundamental issue, wasn't it? Now that his uniform wasn't NYPD blue, it was worn jeans and comfortable shirts. He wore shoes he bought from the mall, he got his boxer briefs in a three-pack and his hair cut for five bucks at the local barber.

Rebecca and him? They were impossible. For a sprint, yeah, okay, but for the distance? No way.

He got into the tub even though there wasn't enough water yet and started massaging his thigh. Later he'd call about adding a therapy session. The muscles around the wound had gotten so damned tight it felt as if with the next step his whole thigh would tear in two. It was impossible to think when it got really bad, and according to the doctor, he was looking at a long rehab. Years. He'd never be the same, but if things went well, he eventually wouldn't have to depend on pain pills to get through a day.

Yet another reason he and Rebecca had a time limit. She could have anyone. The last thing she'd want to be saddled with was some broke ex-cop with no future.

He pressed down on his quadriceps with his thumb, digging into the worst of the pain. It hurt like a wildfire, spreading up, down, throughout his whole body. Why the hell was he even thinking about anything long-term? He had no clue what he was in for. What kind of life he could have, let alone what he wanted.

Rebecca was a slice of fantasy, that's all. He'd check on Keegan, make sure it was his imagination going off the deep end, and then, well, he'd see. She might not want to go out with him again, no matter how great this morning had been. He might wise up and end it before things got more complicated.

By the time he'd finished his soak and taken his damned pill, he'd changed his mind about hitting the computer. Instead, he went downstairs. His dad was in the kitchen, putting a piece of pumpkin pie on a paper plate.

"Did you eat dinner?"

"What are you, my mother?"

"Fine. Get rickets. See if I care. And cut me a piece, would ya?"

Jake reheated a cup of coffee then took both paper plates to the breakfast nook. Mike wheeled himself up to the table and managed his own cup.

"Where'd the boys go?"

He shrugged. "Liam wanted a lift to the mall. He needed some slippers or some damn thing."

Jake shoveled in some pie. "So I'm at this shindig, this party for millionaires, and I hear this guy laugh."

His father didn't look up. Ate. Drank.

"I recognize the laugh. Weird laugh, one you could ID easy, you know?"

The nod was noncommittal, but Jake hadn't gotten anywhere yet.

"The last time I heard it, I was on that joint task force. With the FBI and the ATF?"

"Your guy got away."

"Yeah. It was his laugh. That same weird fucking laugh."

His dad looked up at him. "That's what, a dozen years ago?"

Jake nodded. "I thought it was peculiar especially when I saw this guy from the front. He's got the same build, roughly, but the details are wrong. Hair, nose, eyes, jaw. But this guy, big shot, tons of money. Rebecca's trying to get him to donate a fortune. Anyway, he's got this cleft palate. Sewed up, but the scar is there. Like Stacy Keach."

"Yeah?"

"My guy had a cleft palate. It didn't look as good back then, but come on. The laugh and the lip?"

"Could be a coincidence."

"I know. It's more likely that it's nothing. That I got the laugh wrong. I mean, when's the last time you believed eyewitness testimony? It was years ago."

"He might have been in a fight. Been in a car wreck. Split his lip."

Jake nodded again. Ate some more pie.

"On the other hand," his father said, "you could have identified a fugitive. They had him on a murder charge, right?"

Jake sighed. Sat back and stretched out his leg. "Probably wouldn't hold up now. Evidence gone. Witnesses unreliable from the get-go."

"Might be worth a look."

"You think?" Jake asked, studying his old man's face. No way Mike Donnelly was going to toss him a bone. If Jake was full of crap, his father would say.

"What's your instinct tell you?"

"That he wasn't right."

"There's your answer."

"I could be completely wrong."

"That's true. So take your time. Be careful."

"I'm not a cop anymore."

"Jakey, you'll be a cop till the day you die."

REBECCA WALKED INTO HER condo just after nine-thirty, and she had enough energy to drag herself to her bedroom, strip, leaving her clothes in a heap, and fall into bed.

Things could have gone better at the office. She'd tried, she'd really tried to keep on task, but her thing with Jake had her tied up in knots.

Wasn't love supposed to be all rainbows and unicorns? All she felt was confused. It was supposed to have been a one-night stand. She hadn't meant to get involved with him. He was a wounded ex-cop from Brooklyn. She was…

She was exhausted. And scared. As unsure about what to do as she'd ever been. The idea of not seeing him again hurt. Physically hurt. But if she did see him again, what then? It would just exacerbate the problem. And if they wanted to take it to the next step?

He couldn't leave his father to come live with her. Besides, Jake was a proud man. He wouldn't want to live off her money. She wanted to believe she could become part of his life, but really? Commuting from Brooklyn? Living in a row house?

It was all too much, and her brains were scrambled from the banquet and Jake and the very real possibility that she'd become a person she didn't like very much. But she'd have to deal with it later. Maybe take a few days away from Jake, let things settle. She needed time. And some kind of miracle.

AT TEN-THIRTY, JAKE WAS AT the computer, his coffee fresh, and his leg had simmered down to bearable. There were a lot of hits when he typed in Vance Keegan's name in Google. But each link was about the past, the distant past. The biggest single subtopic was the missing money. They'd been expecting millions, and even the best forensic accountants hadn't been able to trace where all that loot had gone. The press had outdone themselves condemning the police, the FBI and the ATF. A separate task force had been put together to pinpoint the blame, and Jake's anger at reading about it was just as acute as it had been when it had happened.

But this wasn't about history, this was a mission of discovery. He wasn't having much luck. By the time the eleven o'clock news came on, he gave up on finding Keegan and started looking into West. Who was from Nevada. Henderson, born and raised.

The guy was worth a fortune. But he wasn't flashy with it and kept a relatively low profile. He was a venture capitalist who'd made some smart moves, including getting out of real estate before it had all come tumbling down. He was involved with a large number of limited partnerships that specialized in chains, everything from dry cleaning to mortuaries. There weren't a lot of articles about him.

According to the company bio, he was the same age as Keegan. Unmarried, no kids. He'd started his company with profits from a windfall, an inheritance from his uncle, his late father's brother. He'd invested the money, and the rest was a quiet success story.

Nothing hinted that West wasn't exactly who he said he was. But nothing eliminated the possibility either. What was really clear was that Jake didn't have near the access he needed. But he knew someone who could get deeper. A lot deeper.

Gary Summers was an old buddy, a guy Jake had known in college. Gary had been into computers, specifically hacking, since high school. He'd been approached by the government and decided that the good guys had the best toys so he'd signed up. He was an independent bastard, only taking on contract work that interested him. The two of them didn't talk about specifics, and that was probably why they were still friends.

Jake sent him a text. The answer came when he was downstairs helping his old man get ready for the stairs.

Come on up. Next week? Few days? U bring the beer. Send prelim info to 192.175.2.2.

Satisfied for the moment, Jake thought about calling Rebecca, just to hear her voice, but it was late, and he hoped she was sleeping. At the thought, his own exhaustion hit him like a truck. Waking up alone would be a bitch.

12

THE OFFICE WAS QUIET AS A crypt; she should have finished her work hours ago. To make matters worse, it was Sunday, day three of her self-prescribed time-out.

Jake had wanted to see her. He'd asked her to the movies, offered to feed her, even suggested a trip to a real Irish pub. She'd begged off each time, and while her reasons were legitimate, they weren't the whole truth.

Sadly, it turned out time away hadn't made her situation any less confusing. She missed him. Thought of him so often it was absurd. Why was it that even though *she'd* chosen to keep her distance, it felt as if she was being punished? Yearning, it seemed, wasn't just in storybooks, and it had a specific shape and weight right in the center of her chest.

She rubbed her eyes, stretched her neck, then pulled out Jake's trading card to look at his gorgeous face. She thought about her last phone conversation with him. He'd seemed tense. Probably because he could sense she wasn't telling him everything. They'd made love on Thursday morning. They'd bonded intensely, well, she had at least. Based on their phone conversations Jake's world hadn't been rocked off its axis. The two of them hadn't discussed it. By now he probably assumed she was withdrawing since the banquet was over. After she'd seen him in her native environment and found him lacking.

It would be much simpler if that were true.

She should call him.

Rebecca glanced at the clock. Ten minutes had passed since her last check, which had been ten minutes after the glance before. Ridiculous. She picked up the phone and hit speed dial 1. He'd moved up from speed dial 17 on Thursday before her self-imposed exile.

He answered after the first ring. "Hey."

"The thing is," she began, "if I finish answering the emails and writing up the last two reports, I can start tomorrow with a clean slate. All the work from the banquet will be finished on my end."

He paused, then said, "I see. How long do you think that'll take?"

"Longer than it should. I'm in slow motion."

"Any chance you'll be up for a visit at the end?"

Now it was her turn to be quiet.

"Fair enough," he said. "How about this? How about you and me and your clean slate go out to dinner tomorrow night? Early, so that you can get to sleep at a decent hour."

She thought for a second. Seeing him was all she wanted. Also dangerous. Screw it. "That's very doable. In fact, I think it's a great idea. Although, we could eat dinner at home, thereby eliminating a step."

"Tempting," he said, and she could picture him leaning against the wall in the bathroom. The one he was fixing up. She could tell he was in there from the echo. He did like to lean, but that probably had more to do with his bad leg than posing. He'd be wearing his tool belt, too. And jeans. Soft, worn jeans that curved around his most excellent behind.

"Okay," he said. "I'll bring dinner. No cooking. No movie watching. Dinner, then bed."

"Well, that's not going to help me sleep."

"Don't be silly," he said. "We'll have just finished eating. We'll work off dinner. Then you'll collapse in my arms and sleep the sleep of the just."

"Bible quotes?"

"Really?" he asked. "I thought that was from an Elvis Costello song."

She grinned, wanting him with her, right there in the office. Just sitting there so she could look over and see him. He'd smile at her, and she'd get wiggly. Of course then she'd have to go kiss him and her grand plan would bite the dust. "Right. Dinner, my place—"

Another call came on her line, which she would most likely ignore. "Hang on. I'll be right back. It could be work."

She clicked to the second call, a New York number she didn't recognize. "Hello?"

"Rebecca."

William West. She recognized his voice. "Mr. West."

"I thought we agreed on Bill."

"Bill. Can you hold on a moment? I'm on another call."

"I'll wait."

She clicked again, hating that she'd have to put off Jake. If it had been anyone else… "Crap, it is work," she said. "I won't be long. I hope. If it is, we'll talk tomorrow and settle times and stuff, okay?"

"Don't stay up too late. I don't want you falling asleep in the soup."

She smiled and almost blew him a kiss, which...jeez. She was overtired. "Later."

She clicked back to West. "What can I do for you, Bill?"

"I think it's a question of what I can do for you. I'd like to take you to dinner tomorrow evening. We can start the ball rolling on the endowment."

Holy... "Absolutely. Where and when?"

"I'll meet you in front of your office building at eight. The chef at Per Se owes me. We'll have a window seat."

Per Se was one of the most exclusive restaurants in Manhattan, and getting a table there in anything less than six months took an act of congress. "I'll meet you at the car."

Rebecca hung up, looked at her long list of emails, thought about all her options and quickly redialed Jake.

"Yeah?"

"Can you meet me tonight instead? In two hours?"

He was quiet for a minute. "Uh, sure. What changed?"

"William West. He's finally agreed to meet with me tomorrow night to talk actual money. It's not attorneys yet, but it's a major step closer. So I made the executive decision to scrap my noble plans for a clean slate Monday in favor of a delicious Sunday night."

Oddly there was silence again. She'd thought he'd be pleased. "Oh, wait. Is this about your father? We could make it Tuesday night. Give you time to set things up."

"No. No, my dad's fine. He's got friends on standby. Hell, half the neighborhood would volunteer to stay with him if I asked. So, no. It's no problem. I'll bring dinner?"

"That would be excellent."

"You like Chinese?"

"Love it. Especially dim sum. But brunch is probably over, so never mind."

"Never mind? I can get dim sum."

"Really? You're a magician. Oh, that would be... Maybe some extra char siu bao. And har gau. Oh, and spareribs."

Jake laughed. "Is that all? I can just order a couple of everything on the menu."

"I skipped lunch."

"I can't leave you alone for five minutes, can I?" he asked.

The tenderness in his voice made her sit back in her chair. It took her a second to respond, what with swallowing past the lump. "No, I guess you can't. I'll see you in two."

"Don't be late. Your concierge looked hungry the last time I was there."

JAKE WAS THE ONE WHO WAS almost late. Not because of dinner. Gary had called him while he'd been in the cab on the way to the Great Wall restaurant. It wasn't a long conversation, just enough to ruin Jake's mood. He ended up ordering all the dim sum appetizers, even though it was going to cost him a fortune, and he'd have to wait a hell of a long time for it. The wait was fine, and the money, well, he was pretty sure he was trying to prove something by draining his savings, but he couldn't worry about that now. Not when Gary had found something. It didn't necessarily make West a bad guy, but it didn't help.

Rebecca was meeting West tomorrow night. Getting ready to make a deal. What Jake had wouldn't prove anything. The man's laugh reminded Jake of a particular cartoon character. A lot of people were born with cleft palates. If the two things hadn't been combined, he'd have dismissed the notion with barely a second thought. But the two things had been connected.

He had to decide, before he got the food, before he got to Manhattan, whether he was going to ask her to postpone the meeting with West or not.

Dammit, he didn't want this thing with her to be over. Not yet. Yeah, yeah, it was inevitable, like death, like taxes, like his father driving him crazy, but not yet. He might not have a choice about that, though. Something had been off between them the past few days. Ever since Thursday afternoon. It wasn't her workload, that he got completely. She was her job, the way he'd been his, so he had no complaints about the hours she spent at the office. It was more subtle. Pauses when there shouldn't have been. An edginess to her voice.

She'd undoubtedly come to the same conclusion he had, that they were on borrowed time. That the more they saw each other, the more difficult the break would be.

She was the best thing that had happened to Jake in a long time. Even before he'd been shot, his life hadn't been all that spectacular. When he'd been working his way up the ranks, he hadn't wanted a relationship. When he'd gone under, he couldn't have one. And now? With no job, no idea what he was going to do? Even if she wasn't Rebecca Thorpe he'd have no chance in hell.

God, how he'd wanted deep cover assignments. It was always a choice, those, because of what they meant. It was dangerous as hell, obviously, but more than the prospect of being killed, the real long-term danger was getting lost.

He'd been on the edge of doing just that. He'd become Steve "Papo" Carniglia. A wannabe drug lord who'd worked his way up the ranks in the Far Rockaway Gang of Apes, getting close and tight with the man in charge because while he'd acted like a card-carrying member of the Queens' gang, he never played dumb.

As he sat on the really uncomfortable bench waiting for the food, he leaned his head back against the window and cursed his instincts. She had so much riding on West's money. Not just her, but all the people his money could help. The smart thing to do would be to let it go. Forget he'd ever heard that damn laugh. There were a lot of reasons it made sense to put the brakes on, but the one that had him tied up in knots was that she might be walking into something that could put her foundation in jeopardy.

Rebecca was doing everything in her power to elevate the image of the Winslow Foundation, to give it integrity and transparency. If he had a little more time, he could make sure who she was getting involved with. Then they could both rest easy. All he needed was a short reprieve.

He wanted to show her so much. Now that the banquet was over, she'd have time. First thing, he'd take her to the New York she'd never seen. The hidden city he'd spent so long exploring. He wanted to watch her face when she saw where she really lived.

He could have it, too. If she postponed that meeting. Or if he didn't bring up the subject of Keegan at all.

The host called Jake's name, and he shook his head at how overboard he'd gone in buying dinner for two. But he wanted Rebecca to have everything. Food, success, pride, honor, *everything*. How long he had before she came to her senses and showed him the door didn't matter in the end. Nothing mattered except Rebecca.

Well, there was his answer.

SHE OPENED THE DOOR AND laughed out loud when she saw the enormous bags he was carrying. "You dope," she said, taking one of the heavy bags. "You bought the whole restaurant?"

"You skipped lunch."

"Yeah, well, you're taking the leftovers home. That'll feed your dad and his buddies for a couple of weeks."

"Boy, do you not know my dad and his buddies. They may be old, but they eat like beat cops."

She watched him as he hung up his coat. He looked great, as always. No tool belt, dammit, but nice jeans, not quite as worn in, a little darker than the ones she'd declared her favorite, with a white oxford shirt tucked into them. She took another moment to admire his shoulder-to-waist ratio. She was a lucky, lucky woman.

"What's that goofy grin about?"

"You're very attractive," she said.

"That's it? Attractive?"

"That's a lot."

He shrugged.

"I'm not saying that's all you are."

He put his bag on the island, then took the one she was holding and dumped that, too. "What else am I?" he asked as he pulled her into his arms.

"Wow. Fish much?"

"From time to time. Come on." He kissed her, quick, teasing. "Give me something other than looks."

"As if you've never thought hot wasn't reason enough."

"I have, I'll admit it. But you're so much more than that," he said and then he really kissed her. It was as if he'd been starving, but for her. She felt his desperation in his hands and his lips and the way he thrummed with energy. She was helpless to do anything but kiss him back, to give as good as she got. When he finally drew back, she had to blink herself into the present, into the fact that the ache she'd felt for days had dissipated the moment she was in his arms. That she'd never felt like this before, not even dared to dream she could be madly, deeply in love, and that maybe, possibly, he felt... No, he was just being Jake. She'd know if he loved her.

She put some distance between them and the loss of his touch was like a slap. "Let's put out everything on the coffee table and grab whatever. Want a Sapporo?"

He didn't answer for a long minute, and she couldn't read him. Hesitance, and then a smile. His regular smile. "Sure. I'll start unpacking."

Rebecca got the beers, the plates and the good chopsticks. She also brought along her bottle of soy sauce because she had a tendency to squirt the packets all over herself and the furniture.

It looked like a modern sculpture, all the white boxes covering her coffee table. He'd had to put the magazines on the floor and the flowers on the side table.

"I'm going to have one of everything." she said, determined to keep things light. She handed him his beer. "Then decide about seconds."

"You'd better get a move on, because there's only three of each thing."

They sat next to each other on the couch. She had one leg curled under her butt; his legs were spread in that manly way that always amused. After he opened both beers, they grabbed their chopsticks, and it was on.

"Hey," she said, as she opened the third box. You cheated. This is the second box of char siu."

"Actually, I got three orders of those. And two each of the har gau and the ribs."

Before she could even think about it, she kissed him. "Thank you."

He kissed her back, lingering, until he came away with a sigh. "You're welcome. Don't eat them all."

"I wouldn't think of it," she said, deciding right then that the plan to keep her distance was ridiculous. She wasn't going to send him home after they ate. And she wasn't going to kick him out of her bed. Fighting it was a lost cause. Maybe the lesson here was to not be so damn logical about everything. So what if she didn't know where this would lead? That might turn out to be the best part. He'd already taught her so much. Who could say where he would take her next?

They didn't speak for the next while, but she managed to communicate quite well. Mostly by moaning. Taking a bite of the lobster after dipping it into a delicate sauce that was clearly made by the tears of angels, she made loud yummy noises as she chewed.

He laughed at her, looking at her as if she was extraordinary. It was the best dinner she'd had in ages. He stopped eating surprisingly quickly. Probably because he hadn't skipped lunch. Then he got himself another beer, and instead of sitting down again, he stood at the edge of the kitchen, watching her.

She smiled, but it faded after a minute. "I'm sorry about tomorrow night. I can't let this guy slip through my fingers. It's too important."

The words hadn't even finished coming out of her mouth when she saw Jake's demeanor change. His whole body tensed and he frowned, actively frowned.

"What?" she asked. "Are you okay?"

"Yeah. I'm fine," he said, but he burst into motion, leaning over to close the food cartons, avoiding her eyes.

"Jake, what just happened?"

He paused.

"You can't possibly think I have any interest in Bill West outside of his money."

"No. I don't." He stood, abandoning the boxes.

"So?"

"I'd like to ask you to postpone that meeting. With West."

"What? Why?"

He ran his hand through his hair, picked up his empty beer bottle and stared at it for a moment. "I have a bad feeling about him."

"I know. He's not my favorite person either. He flirted with me right in front of his girlfriend, or whoever she was. It was creepy. But I can handle myself."

"That's not it." Jake moved from behind the coffee table and walked over to the window. "Dammit, I wasn't ready to get into this yet."

Rebecca's stomach tightened and it wasn't pleasant. "What are you talking about, Jake? Tell me already."

He stared down into the street for too long before he turned to face her again. "I can't swear to it, but I'm pretty sure I've met West before."

The way he spoke, the way his voice lowered and his eyes grew cold made her very uncomfortable. "And?"

"It was a while ago. Before I did deep cover work. I think I met him at a drug bust."

"He was a junkie?"

"If he's who I think he is, he was a lot worse than that."

"Okay," she said, standing, walking toward him so she could see his face clearly. "I am so not understanding this."

"I have no proof, so this is going to sound crazy. And

I might be wrong. Really wrong. My gut, though. My gut is telling me there's something—"

She shook her head, waiting. Becoming more uneasy by the second.

"I recognized his laugh."

His laugh? She huffed her impatience and gave Jake a look. "Well, okay. It is...unique."

"Yeah. Not easy to forget. But that's not all. The guy I'm thinking of, Vance Keegan, he also had a scar from lip surgery."

"Am I supposed to understand?" she asked.

"No reason you should. He worked for a drug dealer named Luis Packard. A major drug trafficker who ran most of the East Coast for over ten years. Everything from heroin to coke to prescriptions. This guy Keegan was part of the organization, an office guy. Something with the money, although no one ever told me exactly what his role was. They killed a lot of people, sold a lot of drugs to a lot of kids.

"I was in on the bust. It was all over the news because when we were just about to lock it down, Packard's people hit us, hard. Smoke bombs, machine-gun fire. Packard was killed, and so were some of the good guys. The gun that killed Packard had Keegan's prints, among others. Keegan got away. Disappeared. Vanished. They looked for him, but he wasn't on the top-ten most wanted. They were more concerned with where the drug money had gone, all the millions of dollars that were supposedly in a panic room."

He kept talking, and Rebecca stared at him, barely comprehending what was happening. The whole thing was surreal. Jake sounded different, looked different... it was as if she'd stepped into one of their film noirs.

"I always believed Keegan's disappearance and the

missing money were connected. But that whole deal was way above my pay grade. Thing is, I was standing right next to Keegan, and he was laughing that weird laugh as we walked across the roof of the warehouse. He was laughing like he knew something, even though he was cuffed and surrounded by dozens of officers. Then he was gone."

Rebecca took a step back. "You think William West is really Vance Keegan? Wouldn't someone have noticed?"

"He hasn't been in New York in years. He claims to be from Nevada, has a home office there. He travels to Europe, to California, even to Africa and Asia, but he'd never been to New York until a few weeks ago. From everything I read, he's kept himself under the radar until last year. More importantly, he doesn't look the same. I think he had a bunch of surgery, reworked everything from his hairline to the shape of his jaw."

"Wait a minute—you've been investigating him?"

Jake moved a shoulder, his gaze unwavering. "I wouldn't say investigating," he said slowly. "Just searching online."

She had no idea what to do. Jake seemed dead serious. But West had a multimillion-dollar company. There was nothing shady about him, and her people had checked. "Jake, that's really a stretch, not to mention a serious accusation."

"I know. I told you it sounds crazy. And I'm not making an accusation. It's a hunch, but one that needs checking. That's why I'm asking for a postponement. Some time."

She needed some time herself. This was crazy information here, and if it had been anyone but Jake, she'd have laughed and dismissed the whole thing as some weird con. But it wasn't someone else. "I'm pretty certain there is a large percentage of people born with cleft palates."

"They called him Lip," Jake said, nodding. "That must have pissed him off. To be called that by Packard, who was a real piece of work. He was a vicious bastard, ran over anyone trying to get in on his territory. Didn't care who he took out in the process."

"Jake…"

"I know. That's why I decided to do some checking. I couldn't find anything, but my friend… This guy is a genius hacker. Works for Homeland Security. He told me tonight on my way to the restaurant that there's something fishy about the death of West's uncle. That's supposedly how West got his start-up funds. His uncle's estate. But the uncle was murdered. They never found out who did it. There are no other living relatives, and the uncle was a recluse. Lived way out in the desert with the scrub brush and the heat. His body wasn't discovered for almost two months."

Her stomach tightened; she wasn't liking the fact that someone else was involved. If West got wind of any of this… "I'm sorry, I don't see a connection between Keegan and a desert recluse."

"I wasn't gonna say anything. Because I know there are other explanations. I was undercover a long time, Rebecca. I survived by my instincts and training, but trust me, the instincts were more critical. Something clicked for me at the party. Something I can't ignore."

"I see," she said. But she didn't. Jake was wonderful, nearly perfect. But she hadn't even known him two weeks. This? This was kind of scary.

"I only need a week. That's all. Maybe less," Jake mumbled. He turned back to the window and his bad leg wobbled so much his hand shot to the wall for balance.

"But you're right. I'm probably going stir-crazy being stuck at home."

"I didn't say that. Honestly, the thought hadn't even crossed my mind." Unfortunately, it did now. She looked at his taut back, at his image in the mirror. She had the terrible feeling the next few minutes were going to have far-reaching repercussions.

So much for time to think things through. It was all down to *her* instincts now, and while there were many perfectly valid reasons to throw in the towel, and only one for sticking with Jake, she had to bet on the long shot. They might have been together only a short time, but she'd never had a connection like this with anyone. He wasn't crazy. In fact, he was the most down-to-earth, balanced man she'd ever met. Even as she knew her decision was final, she could barely believe it.

She stood behind him, placed her hand on his shoulder. "You're concerned for me," she said.

He faced her, all the ice gone from his gaze. Now his eyes were filled with doubt and fear, a very accurate echo of her own feelings. She couldn't picture a future for them, but she understood what was important to Jake now. Honor. Responsibility. All the things she'd fallen in love with.

"I am concerned for you," he said. "Very much."

"I could postpone, but I won't. Not because I don't believe there's a possibility you might be right. Admittedly, I think it's a very small chance, but anyway, I don't need to postpone because first of all, I'm not in any danger. Second, nothing is going to be signed tomorrow night. This type of deal takes time. The next step is only the negotiation to negotiate."

He nodded, but she doubted he was happy.

"The instant you have any proof, I'll stand with you

and we'll see him put away, but I need to tell you that every person who donates or participates in any meaningful way with the foundation is vetted by our security company. They have remarkable access, which is why they're astronomically expensive. They saw nothing wrong with West's background."

"I'm not surprised. If he did create himself on paper, he would have to have done a remarkably thorough job. I honestly do know how insane this sounds. It would be smarter to let it alone. But I don't think I can."

"Okay. Go with your gut. From what I know about you, I can't imagine you're taking any of this lightly."

He huffed a sad laugh. "So it's not a deal breaker?"

Rebecca ran her hand through his hair. "Nope. And that's why you need to see it through. Because nobody would give this up on a whim."

"Did I hear that right? Did you just tell me you're the hottest woman in New York?"

She laughed. "Now, that would be insane. No," she whispered, then kissed him. "But together, we're pretty incendiary, don't you think?"

His hands were on her now, confident, strong. Running down her back until they curved over her bottom. "Smokin'," he said and he bent to kiss her.

She put up a hand, stopping him. "Please, do not let West get wind of any of this. You have to promise me, Jake. He can't know."

Jake gave her his crooked smile. "You probably won't believe me, but I want to be wrong. I want you to win." Then his mouth was on hers, and she let herself relax against him, let herself trust him. There was an ache inside her and she wanted him badly. The way he'd looked at her, it made her heart hurt. No one had ever looked at her that way before. There'd been lust and hurt and greed and impatience. Even caring and concern and, yes, several kinds of love.

But his gaze had held more than she had words for. This man would slay dragons for her. There was no doubt at all about it. He would put her first over everything.

God, how she wanted him in her bed, in her arms. She wanted to be as close as two people could possibly get. When she tugged his hand, he followed after her, but this time, when they stood by her bed, it wasn't a race. They undressed slowly, one garment at a time, their gazes locked until the last possible second.

When they crawled into bed together, it was quiet. As they gathered each other, wrapping themselves in legs and arms and heat, she felt as safe as she'd ever been.

They kissed. No rush, just kissing. Slow, long touches and rubbing back and forth until the sounds of his breath and her own were only drowned out by the blood rushing in her head, by the beating of her heart.

When he entered her, she stilled him with a cry.

"Rebecca?" he whispered.

"It's good," she said, her lips against his. "Perfect."

13

STANDING OUTSIDE REBECCA'S building at seven-fifteen in the morning, Jake decided to hit a deli a few blocks down, have himself another coffee and try to put his head around what he was getting into.

That she'd made love to him last night, that they'd fooled around in the shower this morning was remarkable, considering, but not nearly as confusing as the fact that she'd made plans with him for Wednesday night. Future plans. When he'd told her his suspicions about West, Jake had seen the growing alarm on her face. He didn't blame her. It would have made so much more sense for her to cut her losses and be done with him.

As if he needed her to be even more incredible. Jesus. Not perfect though. He grinned as he crossed the street, letting the crowd swallow him and set the pace. She'd been cranky as hell this morning. Evidently, all this very fine dining was starting to get to her, and she'd been putting off yoga and the gym because of the donor thing, and she'd declared herself a disgusting slug this morning when her gray wool slacks were harder to zip than they should have been.

His repeated and heartfelt compliments about her

body, complete with kisses and petting, had been dismissed as irrelevant. Because he was a man. So, perfect? No. Which made her even better.

He walked over to 33rd to the 2nd Ave Deli and got himself a booth. He wished he had a notebook or something, but it was more important to have the coffee.

As he waited for the waitress, he tried like hell to organize his thoughts. The first option was to forget about Keegan. Leave it, ignore it. He had the feeling that's the option Rebecca would vote for, despite her support. She'd tell him he was doing the sensible thing. But he rarely did the sensible thing, and this was no exception. It would bother him to the end of his days if he didn't check it out to the best of his ability.

Second option, wait to see what Gary came up with. He knew his friend wasn't infallible, the internet did not have every answer in the world, and the man had a very demanding job. If Gary was discovered looking into anything suspicious, such as the background of William West, it could be bad for Gary.

Jake got his coffee, but before he did anything, he took out his phone. It rang once.

"I don't have anything else for you yet," Gary said.

"Not why I called. How much trouble can you get in for doing this stuff?"

"A lot. If I'm caught. But I won't be. And hell, now that I think of it, not that much trouble. I can always say I found something hinky and was doing my bit for the safety of our great nation."

"Do not bullshit me about this, dude. It's probably nothing. I'd really hate it if you were sent to prison."

Gary laughed. "I don't like you enough to go to prison. Stop worrying about it. I'll call you."

And that was that. Jake fixed up his coffee and as

he stirred, it occurred to him that he had another friend who might be helpful. Well, *friend* was stretching it, but the breakup hadn't been bad…hadn't been terrible at least. Crystal was great, but it was tricky, her being a lawyer and then becoming an assistant district attorney. Thing was, she worked in the Investigative Division of the D.A.'s office. Writing briefs, but still she was inside.

He didn't have her number any longer, but it would be better if he showed up in person, anyway. The one thing Jake had going for him was that he'd never been able to tell Crystal he was an undercover cop. Maybe now that he could, she'd understand why he'd been such a flake. If not, he'd play the sympathy card. She was a nice woman. It would bother her that he'd been shot, even if she had no desire to see him again.

So he'd go to her office. Ask to find out what she could about T-Mac, who was currently serving a life sentence in Sing Sing. He'd been part of the bust, took most of the heat after Keegan vanished and Luis Packard died. There was a chance T-Mac had some information on Keegan's whereabouts, although it was a slim chance.

At least Jake was already in the city. But first, he called his old man.

"You still shacking up with that gorgeous woman?" his father asked.

"Doesn't anybody say hello anymore?"

"Hello. You still shacking up with that gorgeous woman?"

"You're a riot. No. She's gone to work. But I'm gonna be a while. You doing okay?"

"I'm doing fine. The two domino cheaters are here with me, and everything's just peachy."

"Oh, God." Jake lowered his head, not in the least ready to hear about how Pete and Liam were conspiring against Mike to ruin his game. This happened at least once every couple of months and had more to do with the wheelchair knocking over the card table than duplicity and revenge. "You can tell me about it later. You need something for when I come home?"

"No. Yeah. Cookies."

"Chocolate chip or those oatmeal things?"

"Both."

"Maybe you should learn another game. I hear mahjongg is fun."

"Hey, Jakey? Go—"

Jake hung up. Then he got the number for the D.A.'s office and made sure Crystal was there. The odds weren't great that she'd speak to him, but he had nothing to lose. Story of his life.

THE LIMO WAS DIRECTLY IN front of the building, in the red zone; a female chauffeur wearing a traditional uniform opened the back door long before Rebecca reached the sidewalk, and William West stepped out of the car.

He was in a suit; she was sure it cost a bundle, but it wasn't anything special. Didn't particularly flatter him, but that didn't matter. He wasn't on display in this dance. She was.

She smiled and took his hand, then slid onto the seat. A few moments later, he got in on the other side. She'd had just enough time to remember why she was going to this dinner. No matter what ultimately happened, the best information she had right now was that West was a perfectly legitimate businessman who might be willing to donate a significant amount of money to her foundation. Many, many lives depended on those donations, and it was her job to help those people. She would use whatever tactics she believed would get the job done.

That meant manipulating West's attention. She'd be competing with the restaurant, the chef's tasting menu, the unbelievably fine service and the wine. She had to be more fascinating than all of that, and she had to make him feel as if he'd win something big by moving on to the next stage.

Not her. That was never, would never, be on the table, and they both knew that. This parlay was more subtle. It was a conversation. A tease. All about timing. She couldn't afford to think about Jake, about his instincts, about her feelings. Tonight she was fighting for inoculations, for clean water, for medical care, for food, for women and children.

"It's great to see you again so soon," West said. "I enjoyed the banquet, but this is even nicer, don't you think? A chance to get to know one another."

"It will be nice. I've been looking forward to it all day."

"Good. I called ahead. The chef's tasting menu tonight sounds fantastic."

"You know him?"

He nodded. "We've crossed paths."

"I didn't think you got to the city very often."

"Chef Keller travels to Las Vegas frequently."

"Ah, of course."

It was quiet for the rest of the drive, which wasn't long. Then they were at The Time Warner Center at Columbus Circle, and she was being escorted to the fourth-floor restaurant.

As soon as they were inside, the mâitre d' greeted them both by name. West walked behind her to take her coat. As it came away, she heard his soft gasp as he realized her dress was backless. Very backless. She allowed herself a tiny smile.

They were led to a window table with a gorgeous view of Central Park. She liked the restaurant, who wouldn't, as it was owned and run by the chef of the French Laundry, but the nine-course meal, even with tiny portions, was almost more than she could deal with after the week she'd had. It would have been so much better to be at Jake's place in Brooklyn, listening to his dad and friends, watching something on TV and eating a simple salad.

But she followed the rules of engagement. Nods at the wine, smiles and questions, letting him do most of the talking until the sixth course. She'd been judicious whereas West had been quick to refill his glasses of wine, different kinds, perfectly paired with each delicacy.

She excused herself, sure his gaze never left her back as she went to the ladies' room. Once there, she relaxed. It was just as elegant as one would expect. Spacious, beautiful, quiet. When she returned to the table, she'd get down to business, and she would get him to commit to a dollar amount.

So far she'd seen nothing suspicious about the man. He wasn't the most refined person she'd ever met but he wasn't in any way vulgar. He had no accent, not even a trace of New York. His laugh gave her chills, though she hadn't reacted, but she'd had to force her gaze away from his mouth more than once.

He rose as she approached the table on her return, then held her chair for her. As she was sitting, he bent in such a way that the light hit the edge of his hairline. That was when she saw it. A scar at his hairline, artfully masked by his dark hair. She'd seen enough face-lifts to know what she was looking at, and while it could be a remnant of his vanity, it might be something else completely.

As they continued on with little plates of perfect food, and talk swung to the endowment itself, she watched his face. Jake had said his jaw was different. Those scars were tricky, and not all could be hidden.

By course nine, she had him talking about five million a year for ten years. And she'd identified scar tissue just below his right ear.

That still meant nothing; half of her parents' friends had had work done. Although she'd apparently been giving him the wrong signals by watching him so carefully. The way he looked at her now spoke of a deal that had nothing to do with charity.

JAKE HADN'T EVEN TRIED TO sleep. It was eleven-thirty and he was bone tired but he was pacing the house like a caged animal. He hadn't asked her to call. But he couldn't imagine she wouldn't. She knew he was worried. The dinner probably wasn't over yet, so he should calm the hell down.

What he needed to do now was prepare himself. She had a lot riding on this deal. No reason for her to believe everything wasn't completely kosher, and if West had offered to give the foundation a ton of money, Rebecca would be pleased. And he'd be pleased for her.

Until proven guilty, West was nothing more than a victory for her and her foundation, and Jake could damn well keep anything else out of the conversation.

The TV was off, his old man was in bed, the place was quiet and Jake debated going to Midtown, waiting for her at her place. He dismissed the idea as beyond stupid, but man, he wished like hell she'd call.

He could call her. She'd know why. She was smart,

she was amazing, she'd be onto him in seconds. And she'd think he'd gone from being slightly nuts to tin-hat crazy.

He thought again about his afternoon at the D.A.'s office. He had no idea if it was going to pay off or not, but in the end it didn't matter what Crystal found out. He had already made arrangements with Pete to borrow his 1970 Barracuda. The car was the only thing, aside from dominoes and his friends, that Pete gave a crap about, and that he had given Jake the keys with no hesitation said a lot. That was one part of being home that had been great to relearn.

Of course cops watched out for each other, but when you're in deep cover, it was different. Any association with other law-enforcement personnel was dangerous for everyone involved. Jake hadn't realized just how empty his life had been for far too long. Filling it again was a privilege. He'd done pretty well with home and family. But that still left a lot of room.

Although it would play hell on his leg, he limped down the hall and grabbed his jacket. He wouldn't be gone long. He didn't like leaving his father alone, but Mike rarely woke up once he conked out. There was no reason for his father to go downstairs even if he did.

Soon, if Jake could ever get his life back on track, Mike wouldn't have to worry about stairs. Yet another reason this thing with Rebecca wasn't the best of ideas. Jake had his responsibilities at home and until he could figure out another way, that meant sticking close to Brooklyn.

He walked toward Fifth, taking his time, trying not to focus on his thigh but on his destination. There was a bar where a man could buy a beer. One beer, then he'd come back, get himself ready for bed.

When his cell rang in the middle of Howard and 4th, he jumped and grabbed for it so fast he almost dropped the damn thing. "Hello?"

"Did I wake you?"

Jake relaxed. Rebecca sounded good. Tired, but good. "I'm up. You okay?"

"He has some scars."

"What?"

"Scar tissue. One could have been from a face-lift, but there were several more, hard to see, and I might be wrong. I tried to dismiss it. I know a lot of people who've had work done, but I'll admit it's bothered me because it was a lot of scar tissue. It was behind his ear, but it wasn't like a face-lift scar. You said his jaw had been altered."

"Yeah, that's what I thought. The jaw, the nose, the hairline and his eyes."

"They weren't easy to spot. He had an amazingly good surgeon. And God knows a cosmetic scar isn't proof, or half my relatives would be arrested."

"No, they're not proof. But I may be able to get something more tomorrow. I'm taking Pete's car up to Sing Sing."

"Where's that?"

"Ossining. About an hour and a half drive. I'm going to visit one of the men who was working with Keegan. See what he can tell me."

"You're not a cop anymore," she said, and he could hear the soft movements of cloth against cloth. "Can you just show up like that?"

"I know a guy who knows a guy. Professional courtesy and all that. It shouldn't take too long. He'll either talk or not, but I figure he might be pretty unhappy to be sitting in jail while Keegan's out and about making so much money he can afford to give it away."

"If it's Keegan." She sounded tense.

"Right. If." He didn't feel much like getting that beer now so he turned around. "And if he's William West, how did your meeting go?"

"Look, Jake, you can't mention West's name tomorrow. Ask all you want about Keegan, but promise me you won't try linking him to West."

"I won't. I never planned to. You have my word."

She sighed with relief. "Jesus, you've got me all crazy and paranoid now."

He winced. Her words took a chunk out of him but he sucked it up. He couldn't blame her for not blindly jumping on the bandwagon. "Okay, for now we're assuming everything's copacetic with West. Tell me about dinner."

"It went well. There's the chance we'll be getting five million a year for ten years."

Jake whistled. "That's not chump change."

"I'm not holding my breath about it. There's a lot that could still fall apart on this deal. The foundation will go on, one way or another."

"I'm just glad you're okay."

"I am," she said. "Oh, and Jake?"

"Yeah?"

"You're considerate. Charming. Sexy. Funny. Decent. Dedicated. Heroic. Did I mention sexy?"

He laughed. "What's that about?"

"Last night you asked me what I liked about you. Aside from you being so very, very good-looking."

"I see," he said, flushing under the cold light from the streetlamp, glad she hadn't thrown in that he was nuts. "That was quite a list."

"All true."

"Sure you haven't mistaken me for an Eagle Scout?"

"Positive."

"Damn, woman. I wish you were a whole lot closer."

"Be glad I'm not. I'm so tired I can barely see. Do me a favor, check in with me tomorrow. I don't want to worry that you've been trapped in some prison riot or something."

"Okay. I will. And Rebecca? You're pretty goddamn fantastic yourself."

For a minute, he listened to her breath. "Good night, Jake. Drive safely. Be careful. Come back in one piece."

"I promise."

14

THE BARRACUDA WAS A BEAST in terms of power, but one hell of a beauty to drive. Now that Jake was almost at the prison, he turned down the factory-installed AM radio and went over his plan of action.

Crystal had come through, thankfully. She'd called him this morning with T-Mac's prison records and more importantly an overview of his phone records. Some of his calls had been from and to lawyers, but he had family. A mother and sister in Georgia. They didn't come by, only called. No calls to or from Nevada. As for T-Mac's life inside, he'd gone with the Bloods, which wasn't a surprise considering, and he wasn't classified as a high-risk inmate. He'd been there eleven years, time enough to get established, but not quite time enough for a chance at parole. They'd never been able to pin a murder on T-Mac.

His real name was Lantrel Wilson, and Jake had no idea where T-Mac had come from or what it meant. He'd been associated with Packard as a kid. Been arrested for selling drugs to other kids and sent to a juvenile facility three times before he was seventeen. He'd been thirty-four when he was busted in that raid, and according to testimony, which was highly suspect as it was given by other members of Packard's operation, T-Mac was not just an office guy, he was one of only three or four people who had access to the panic room safe.

The signs warning against picking up hitchhikers popped up frequently as he continued on toward Hunter St., the icy-blue Hudson to his left.

Then there was the rigmarole about getting inside. Crystal had come through on that, too, and he owed her now. Flowers. Expensive flowers. He kept his eyes and ears open as he went through check after check until he was finally admitted into one of the cubicles they used for attorney visits. It took fifteen minutes for the door to open, and T-Mac was led inside.

First eye contact was definitely a challenge, but this wasn't Jake's first rodeo so he ignored it, using the silence to note the changes eleven years had wrought. The man had some serious muscle now. Enough tattoos to decorate the cubicle walls a couple times over. And that was only what Jake could see. T-Mac wore his long hair in cornrows that looked greasy, had a Van Dyke beard and squinty little eyes.

"Who the fuck are you?" he asked, finally.

"You can't guess?"

"Cop?"

Jake smiled. "Ex-cop."

"So? What you want?"

"What can you tell me about Lip?"

T-Mac didn't blink. He looked uncomfortable, but that might have been because his chair was too small for his bulk. He could barely cross his arms. "Who?"

"Hey, you're the one that ended up taking the fall for Packard, for Lip, for everything. I would imagine

Lip getting away scot-free would be something to think about over the years."

"You don't know what I think about."

"I do not. You're correct. But I would like to find out what you know about Vance Keegan."

"For all I know, he's dead and gone. I got no word about him from nobody. Not for all the time I been here."

"Nothing? Not a sighting? Say, from someone in Nevada?"

That got Jake a wince and a look. "You think I got pen pals or somethin'? How'd you even get in here, ex-cop? What are you looking for?"

"I'm writing a book."

"Yeah, and I'm singing in a choir. That all?"

"I don't know. I have to wonder, though, if it turned out that Lip wasn't dead. That he was, say, living it up on the money that was supposed to be in the panic room. Making more money off that. Spending money. A lot of it. Would that clear up your memory some?"

"What the hell you talking about? Lip was nothing. Nobody. He got coffee and set up hookers."

"Yeah. That sounds about right. Packard. He was a real sonofabitch, wasn't he? Charging his own people twenty-percent interest? That had to sting."

That got a reaction. It had been a rumor, a note on a piece of paper that Crystal had found.

"It's time you left, ex-cop. I got nothing to say to you."

"Nothing to pass on if I should miraculously discover Lip is alive and well?"

T-Mac gave him a contemptuous look, then stood up. Jake found it was a lot faster to get out of the prison than in. Just as well…the trip had been nothing but a big waste of time.

IT FELT AS IF REBECCA hadn't been to the St. Marks church kitchen in months. Although they would meet next Monday to exchange lunches, today was a special gathering, a birthday party. Two women, an account rep for MetLife and a personal assistant of a famous author, were turning thirty. Rebecca couldn't always make it to the group get-togethers, but she'd been delighted to come to this one. Not only did she like Ally and Tricia, but left to her own devices while Jake was at the prison, she would have been a wreck.

It was too soon to expect a call, but she'd been on tenterhooks the whole morning. Her day, in fact, had been terrifically normal. Flowers delivered from Bill West, thanking her for the dinner. No meaning to it, just something men tended to do when they wanted to get into someone's pants. Or just to be polite, but that's not what West's gesture had been about. He wanted more. The way he'd looked at her at the end of the evening? It was as if he was doing everything in his power to figure her out, right down to how she liked her coffee in the morning. It had been an uncomfortable ride home, but maybe that was just her. What she knew about him, suspected about him, colored her perspective once the business of the evening had ended.

There was no proof. It was highly unlikely that he was a wanted man, a killer. If she eliminated that possibility entirely, what she was left with was a guy from Henderson, Nevada, who'd made a bundle and felt he wasn't getting enough attention. Or not enough attention from the right people. Why else come to New York to contribute his millions? He could have easily found worthy causes in Vegas or California.

No, he was looking for validation. He'd taken her to Per Se to impress her. That's why he'd brought a date to the banquet. He was preening, and that should have been her only consideration until there was more to go on than a couple of scars and an odd laugh.

"Well?"

Katy Groft stood in front of Rebecca. She'd changed her hair color to a softer brown with caramel highlights. It really suited her.

"You mean Jake."

"Yes, I mean Jake. How was it?"

"Great," she said, catching herself in the nick of time. Katy had gone out with Jake, too, and what was the proper etiquette for disclosure in the trading card world? She didn't know Katy that well. It might hurt her feelings that Jake and Rebecca had hit it off. Or she might be delighted. "He's a really nice guy."

"Nice guy, hell. He's gorgeous and funny and smart. He's the best date I've had this year. Wish it could've lasted longer with him, but *c'est la vie*."

Rebecca gave it up as a lost cause and told the truth. "You know what? Me, too. Best date in years. He's pretty amazing."

Katy stepped back two paces. "Oh," she said. "Why do I get the feeling it wasn't only one night with you two?"

Rebecca felt the warmth of her blush and was thrilled when she saw Bree approach. The lunch brigade were filing in now, and things would get moving soon. The cake was here, along with all the accoutrements. Instead of gifts, everyone was donating to the St. Marks kitchen, which, in addition to letting them cook, also served weekend meals to people in need. "It's been several more," she admitted. "And we're getting together tomorrow night."

"No," Katy said, her voice dropping low and loud. "You are kidding me."

"What?" Bree asked, not the least abashed by nosing in on the conversation. "Are we talking about Jake?"

"You know about Jake?" Katy asked.

"Met him. He's a dream. I swear, if I wasn't with Charlie—"

"You're still with Charlie Winslow?"

All three women turned at that voice. It was Shannon, of Hot Guys New York trading card fame, making her entrance with her usual flair, red hair flying, high heels clicking across the floor. "I should have charged money for these cards. The hits keep on coming."

"It was a stroke of genius," Bree said. "You should call the *Times*. Have them do an article."

Shannon gasped, her eyes wide and shocked. "No one is calling anyone, especially not the media. God, can you imagine? Men would be climbing all over themselves to get on the cards. And they'd all want to show off their *assets,* if you know what I mean." She held up her hand, index finger and thumb about two inches apart.

"Either that or they'd be lining up to sue you," Lacy said with a laugh.

Shannon shook her head. "For a dating circle? No one has that much free time."

"Besides," Katy said, "men are too vain. None of them would complain about using their pics without permission, especially if it got them on a date with one of us."

"Your lips to God's ears," Shannon said, with a glance toward the ceiling. "I want to keep playing with the deck. I'm certain I'm going to meet my Mr. Right through this plan. It's fated." She flipped her hair over her shoulder. "So let's all remember to keep this our little secret."

Rebecca grinned, but she agreed with Shannon in principle. The whole reason the trading cards worked was because it was a controlled environment. "Well, I'm thrilled that I'm part of it," she said. If Shannon couldn't get accolades from the press, she certainly deserved them from her. "I'm seeing someone really special."

"I didn't think we had any more gazillionaires in the stack," Shannon said. "Or was he posing as a regular guy?"

That stung. A lot. "No, he is a regular guy."

"Oh." Shannon frowned. "I'm sorry. I didn't mean—"

"Yes, you did. But it's okay. No reason not to. I was as surprised as anyone."

"Come on," Bree said, bumping her shoulder. "You're not like that. I'd know."

"No, I'm not looking for an escape clause," Rebecca said, touching Bree's hand. "I've had to do some real soul-searching over this. I never realized how accustomed I'd become to men of a certain class. It's been a real wake-up call. Yet another reason to be grateful for the trading cards."

Shannon wasn't frowning now. Her face softened, and her very pink lips curved into a smile. "That's good," she said. "Thank you for telling me that."

"I can't believe I let him get away," Katy said. "I had him first."

"You said it was all right."

Katy grinned at Rebecca. "Of course it's all right. I'm kidding. Jealous, but kidding. Now, return the favor and set me up with someone wonderful."

"I'll do my best," she said. She would, too. But there

wasn't a single man in her life, now that Charlie was taken, that she'd want to share with the women here. Her friends deserved better.

HE PULLED INTO A GAS STATION in Englewood to fill up the Barracuda. It took premium gas, for God's sake, and it drank like a lush. But, oh, how Pete loved this car.

Jake wasn't sure why—maybe he hadn't gotten the car gene—but he'd never been into them. Not even when he'd gotten his driver's license. He'd bought an old Toyota when he had enough money, learned enough to change the oil, change plugs and points, the basics, and that was fine. It was lucky he'd been a decent quarterback because he'd been harassed about that old bucket of bolts from day one.

Instead he'd become obsessed with guns. Not rifles, although he could handle one. Not hunting, he had no interest. He'd learned about guns at the shooting range, on a Smith & Wesson 36 revolver. He and his father had been like most teenagers and their dads, arguing, pissing each other off about everything, his hormones in charge, his father's patience stretched beyond the limit, but not at the range. There, Mike had been an extraordinary teacher, and Jake, an obedient and helpful son. That had lasted until Jake got two more bull's-eyes than his old man.

After he'd spent an ungodly amount on gasoline, Jake pulled the car into an empty space at the little food market, far from where anyone else would park. He was more afraid of wrecking Pete's car than he was of that prison riot Rebecca had warned him about.

He got himself a soda, found a seat on a bench where he could watch the Barracuda, which was worth a lot of money, not to mention Pete's well-being, and called Rebecca.

"Hi," she said. She sounded relieved, and that made him feel better than he'd expected, considering. "How did it go?"

"As far as concrete information? It sucked. But if you count inferences that could lead directly to the next step in the process, it also sucked."

"Oh, no," she said, but he could hear the relief in her tone. She probably assumed the poking around was over. That West was exactly who he said he was. She might be right.

"T-Mac wasn't forthcoming," he said. "The only undertone I got from him was his distinct wish that I would die. Soon."

"But I thought he was the one who got slammed with the whole deal." Rebecca sighed, and he could hear a murmur of voices in the background. "Wasn't he angry?"

"I couldn't tell. Probably. But then, the man's in prison for a hell of a long time. I don't think he has a lot of up days."

"No, I mean, shouldn't he have been more angry? Considering?"

It was Jake's turn to sigh. "I thought of that. But even if that's the case, there's nothing to do with the information. For all I know, Keegan's dead, T-Mac is just a guy in the joint and Packard had spent every last penny on a massive comic-book collection. I've got nothing."

"But you tried."

"Is that laughter I hear? Are you having fun while I'm moping?"

She giggled. "I'm at St. Marks. It's a birthday party, and it's almost over. I have to get back to the office."

"Ah, the frozen lunches. Put those together with the leftover dim sum, and you won't need to shop for a month."

"Ugh, food is the last thing I'm interested in. No lunches today though, only cake and ice cream. You want to come over tonight? Though it can't be too early because I have a meeting."

He was flat out grinning now. Had been since she'd said hello, for that matter, but that last question? That had been something else altogether. "I do," he said, tempted. No, he wasn't going to risk ruining his plan for tomorrow night. His leg had to be in full working order. "But I don't think I should."

"Oh?"

"I know it's very unmanly, but the truth is I'm exhausted. I need to do some work on my poor wounded body then get myself a full night's sleep. I won't do that if I'm with you."

"I give a pretty good massage."

Shit, her persistence was killing him, but did he want her to see how bad his leg was today? "Sweetheart, there is no way in the world I'm going to be in a bed with you and not keep us both up. Besides, you need to rest, too. I'm taking you somewhere special tomorrow evening."

"Where?"

"It's a surprise."

"No fair," she said, almost whining, which was pretty damn adorable. "Tell me."

"Nope. Wear something warm and comfortable. None of those lethal high heels."

"You like it when I wear high heels."

"Only when you're not wearing anything but your fancy underwear."

She didn't say anything for a minute. He could tell

she'd gone somewhere more private, quieter. "I'm sorry things didn't pan out about West. I'm happy for the foundation… You know what I mean."

"Yeah, I do. Although I'm not totally ready to throw in the towel. Unless that's what you want."

"How about we keep thinking it through," she said, her voice warm and sexy. "Who knows, together, we might come up with something that'll not only uncover the truth, but find all that missing money. Then I can negotiate a reward for the foundation."

He laughed. She really was good. "Yeah. Okay. We'll keep thinking. And if we don't uncover squat, we'll have given it a hell of a shot, right?"

"So tomorrow?" she asked.

"I'll pick you up at seven. Does that work?"

"Seven's great. Hey, Jake?"

"Yeah?"

"Sleep well. Take care of yourself."

"I…"

"Yeah?"

"Nothing. Thanks. You sleep well, too." He hung up his phone and stared at it as he took another big swig of soda. By the time he put the cell back in his pocket and climbed back into the car, he knew exactly how much trouble he was in.

He'd fallen for her. Fallen like a kid off a bicycle. Shit, he was in for a world of hurt.

15

WHOEVER THE HELL HAD invented full-length mirrors deserved to be sent to the same level of hell as shoe designers. The jeans Rebecca had on now were tight and made her look thinner, yet when she took them off they left a red indent around her waist, which Jake would see. Unless she wore a teddy under and didn't take that off until the lights were out and, oh, hell. Why was she so nervous?

She sucked it up to unzip, then traded the jeans for a different, looser pair. The solution to the whole problem turned out to be not looking in the mirror. Simple.

As per his instructions, she'd put on comfy boots that had virtually no heels at all, and a wonderful thick sweater she'd gotten for skiing. She had no idea where he planned to take her that would require walking in the cold March air, but for his sake she hoped there were plentiful rests and a nice place to snuggle when they got there.

The buzzer from the front desk caught her finishing her lipstick and speeded up her heart. She didn't even know how it could be more exciting to see him now than it had that first night. But it was. He made her pulse race, her insides tighten and her nipples get hard. What a fantastic superpower.

She couldn't even wait for the elevator to bring him up. Instead she stood outside by her open door, impatient and grinning.

At the sound of the ding she rose up on her toes, but settled before he stepped clear of his ride. His grin matched hers in intensity, and they sort of rushed at each other. It would have been ridiculous except for the kiss. That trumped everything. His hand cupped the back of her neck and she sneaked inside his coat to take hold of his hips. She pulled him in close so they were smooshed together thigh to chest and she filled herself up with his scent.

He went on kissing her, tasting her, the two of them greedy and eager as teenagers. When he moaned low and pushed his budding erection against her, she wondered if maybe they should skip the surprise and stay in bed for the next ten hours or so.

When he broke the kiss, he didn't go far. His forehead touched hers as he slowly exhaled, fingers still rubbing soft circles on her nape. "That was some welcome."

"Yeah, well, I love surprises."

"So it's the idea that's important, huh?" he asked. "For all you know I could be taking you for a pushcart falafel in the Village."

"It would depend on the cart." She needed to look at him. Still, she was disappointed when his hand fell away from her nape. "Come on, where are we going?"

"Get your coat. I'll show you."

She took hold of Jake's hand and led him into the house. Her coat and purse were ready. "You need to make a pit stop? Grab something to drink?"

He shook his head, his crooked smile melting her into a puddle of goo. "You continue to amaze me," he said.

She stopped short. "What? Why?"

"You surprise me every time we get together. Every time."

"How am I surprising you now?"

"You're like a kid on Christmas. I don't want to disappoint you. We're not going to Paris or anything."

She put her stuff back down on the table and walked to him. Hands on his shoulders made him look her straight in the eyes. "I don't care where we're going. Pushcart, Paris. Doesn't matter. I just want to hang out with you. And then screw like bunnies when we get back."

"Ah. I see. I hadn't thought of the screwing like bunnies part. I think I can change the itinerary. Anything for a friend."

"So, I'm a sacrifice now?"

He shook his head slowly. "You're the best thing that's ever happened to me." His voice had deepened and she heard him swallow, as if he hadn't meant to say that out loud.

She had to kiss him. Had to. She tried to make him see it was okay what he'd said. It was more than okay. Without scaring the pants off him. Or herself.

She was his best thing. She'd never been anyone's best thing before.

Wow.

JAKE TOOK HER HAND AS HE scooted into the cab beside her. "Brooklyn Bridge Station, please."

The cab took off, making its winding way to Broadway. Rebecca leaned against the window, the neck of her wool coat turned up, framing her face perfectly. "Brooklyn Bridge Station? Hmm."

"You won't guess."

"Let me think. What's around there?" She closed her eyes, and he wanted to kiss her. "It's the Financial District, so Bridge Café?"

"Naturally, you're going to think of restaurants. We're not going to a restaurant."

"Simply narrowing down the field." She grinned and fluttered her lashes at him, as if that had been her plan all along. "The Woolworth Building? South Street Seaport?"

"You're getting warm, but no. Not where we're going."

"New York Academy of Art?"

"How do you even know that?" he asked.

"Went to a fundraiser there. Oh, City Hall. Municipal buildings. Courts and things, right?"

"Yes. That's it. I'm taking you to courts and things."

She sighed as they waited in the crushing traffic. "I give up."

"Good. I bet you were hell on Christmas. Did you always find where your folks had hidden your gifts?"

Her smile faded a little. "No. Christmas wasn't like that at our house. My grandparents were taught to keep a rein on their emotions. That was a point of pride, and it was passed on. Drummed in. The trees were decorated by professionals. Christmas dinner was catered. I got mostly sensible gifts. Clothes, books. Charitable donations were made in my name."

"Wait. When you were a kid?"

She nodded. "Not only me. My cousins, too. It wasn't a horrible message. We'd been born into privilege and with that came responsibilities. When we were very young, we had chores around the house, and as soon as we were able, we were expected to do volunteer work in one form or another. It wasn't optional."

"But what about being a child? What happened to that part?"

"That was where Charlie came in. He was, just so you know, the devil incarnate. A rebel even in kindergarten. He gave me my first cigarette at eleven. Let's see. He helped me steal my first candy bar from a Duane Reade drugstore. We used to sneak into the liquor cabinets during the parties our parents would host and get absolutely smashed. I'm not sure why the nannies never busted us. I think they were glad to see us letting off steam. My family and his were really close, did everything together, until they caught us ditching school. We'd gone to Atlantic City when we were in seventh grade. I only saw him a couple of times a year after that. Well, officially. Unofficially, he remained my hero and we sneaked out all the time."

"I knew I liked him right off the bat."

"His parents were at the donor dinner."

"I didn't meet them."

"That's okay," she said. "They're…rigid. And the honest and horrible truth is, I don't think they like Charlie. Which is a shame because he's really something."

"I'm glad you had each other."

"Me, too. But when it came down to choosing what I was going to do with my life, the lessons of my parents had the most impact. I set my sights on the Winslow Foundation. We're doing good things."

He leaned over, helpless not to kiss her. "I was brought up the same way. Kind of."

"Yeah, I got that," she said, brushing her fingers over his cheek.

They swayed together with the stops and starts of the taxi. Rush-hour traffic was never easy. But that was okay. He was fine where he was. Jake brushed her lips with his one more time. "I never wanted to be anything but a cop. My family was full of heroes. I grew up believing that I could make a difference. I still do. My father, he was a tough sonofabitch. He didn't let me get away with much. But he worked like a dog to make sure I got into college, got my degree before I joined the force. I think he was hoping I'd grow up to be chief of police or something. I never wanted that. I needed to be on the street."

"You're pretty tough yourself."

"I was. I helped put away some bad people. I never took kindly to those bastards preying on the weak and the helpless. They destroyed families, kids. It was frustrating, because we'd get rid of one operation and another would take its place in a heartbeat. But you can't let that stop you. You do what's in front of you."

Rebecca's face was half in shadow, but he could see that she was staring at him, not grinning now, not moving. Just looking at him. "I admire you, Jake Donnelly. I admire your values and your courage and your willingness to take a stand."

He was pretty sure she couldn't see his blush. "I honored the job. Like my father did, and his father."

"Did you know you have a Brooklyn accent when you talk about your dad?"

"Is that so?"

"Yep." She leaned in, but the cab veered to the left and came to a jarring stop. "Brooklyn Bridge Station."

Jake had gone to the ATM before he'd picked up Rebecca, and even though he had to quit this crazy spending, he'd taken out a few hundred bucks. Just in case.

He paid the cabbie, then helped her out of the taxi. Now came the good part. It was brisk out, but not freezing. The air smelled clean for New York, and once they got free of the subway entrance, the street traffic thinned. "You ready to go on an adventure?"

"Oh, God, yes. Lead on, Macduff."

He grinned wide. "It's actually 'Lay on, Macduff.' But don't feel bad. It's misquoted all the time."

"I stand corrected," she said with a little bow.

He tried to leave it at that, but he couldn't. "That was on *Jeopardy* the other night."

She laughed and shook her head. "It still counts."

"Good." He took her hand again. "Follow me." He could have asked the cabbie to drop them closer to their ultimate destination, but he wanted it to be a surprise until the last minute. There was no rush. He'd accomplished what he'd needed to last night. Soaked for a long time, done the massage work, then he'd seen his physiotherapist for a session this morning. He'd needed it. Because tonight the pain was under control and his limp wasn't as noticeable. He figured he could get through the next couple of hours, no sweat.

Finally, in City Hall Park they came to another subway entrance: City Hall Station. When he pulled her to a halt, she gave him a sidelong glance. "Why did we go to the Brooklyn Bridge Station when we were coming here?"

"Because the subway doesn't stop here anymore. Well, that's not completely true. A train does come here, but only to turn around and leave again."

"Explain, please?"

"Let's explore the park. Do you mind?"

"Never. Adventure. Surprise. What could be better?"

She got closer to him, switched from holding his hand to putting her arm through his.

"In 1904, this was one of the first terminals of the IRT. This particular station was built as a showpiece. The city elders went all out. It was gorgeous, but it had two things that didn't work so well. One, not many people needed this stop when the Brooklyn Bridge platform was so close. Two, the trains back then were shorter than they are now, and the tracks here were configured in a pretty tight loop."

He led her to the park fountain, circled by flickering gas oil lamps, which made the water look magical. He pointed. "These are reconditioned lamps from the late nineteenth century, although some of them have been updated a little."

Jake watched Rebecca, her chin up, eyes wide as she took in the details of the old lighting fixtures. It was remarkably quiet around them, the swooping and falling of bursts of water onto the granite base of the fountain masking the traffic noise. He'd seen only a couple of people rushing across City Hall Park.

He was excited; he could feel his blood pumping and his adrenaline spike. He loved New York, especially Manhattan, and he'd become an urban explorer when he had time off, although he hadn't been able to do a lot of that since the shooting. He wanted her to see the hidden treasures all around her, and of course, it had to begin with City Hall Station.

He tugged at her arm and walked her around some greenery toward a circular tablet embedded in the sidewalk in the south end of the park. Most people never noticed it as it wasn't well lit at night. But he'd prepared for that. He pulled out a flashlight to better illuminate it. There were carvings in the center, a time line of the history of City Hall, including the abandoned subway station.

"There used to be a big post office building here. They called it Mullet's Monstrosity. It was on Mail Street, which didn't survive."

He moved the flashlight to the right. "That's where it used to be. There's more than one street that vanished," he said. "Tyron Row disappeared, too. Park Row, where we are, is the only street in New York City called a row."

She crouched down, staring at the careful workmanship. "I love this. How many times have you been here?"

"More than I can count. I started exploring the old places when I was in college. A friend of mine who works for the IRT calls himself an urban historian. He's got a great blog. And something far more important."

She rose again and looked at him instead of the view. "What's that?"

"Keys to the kingdom."

"Where are you taking me, Jake?"

"Back in time," he said, then pulled her along, anxious now to retrace their steps to the subway entrance. They were still in City Hall Park though, and he didn't rush her because this part was good. It was great to have her outside, not at a restaurant, no parties, no pressure. From what he could tell, she was enjoying herself. Interested. There was so much to tell her, too. But tonight was something extraordinary. He was taking her for a private tour of the old City Hall subway station, refurbished for the 2004 centenary, but closed to the public. Tours were available, and they were fun, but he wanted the two of them to be alone for this.

"Huh," Rebecca said. "I don't even know what IRT stands for. I've lived here all my life, and I don't know that. I mean, obviously Rapid Transit."

"Interborough," he said. "Right around here was the start of subways in New York. The groundbreaking ceremony was held in 1900 and this platform opened in 1904."

She turned to face him. "I think this calls for a moment, don't you? Something to celebrate?"

"What did you have in mind?"

She looked up at him, her lips already parted. The kiss started slow. More breath than lips at first, then a brush, a tease. Jake let her run the show. Standing in the shadows, she was the tour guide now, and she seemed to know every important stop along the way, mapping his mouth with deliberate care, then begging entrance with a moist nudge. Of course he obliged. He wasn't a fool. And God, she tasted like everything he wanted.

He ran his hands underneath her coat, wanting to pull her blouse out of her pants so he could touch her skin, but if he did that, the tour would be over. She compelled him like that, made him want too much. But that had been true from the moment he'd set eyes on her. He couldn't get enough.

Her fingers slid up the back of his scalp and he gripped her tighter. The pressure kept building inside him, but he couldn't break away, not completely. Not yet. His mouth went to her jaw, her neck, and he kissed her there where he could breathe her scent and trail his tongue up to the shell of her ear.

"Wait," she said, stepping away. "Whoa. I'm getting a little carried away here."

He nodded, catching his breath, willing his heartbeat to slow.

"I really want to see the surprise," she said. "So here's the rule. No more fooling around until later. Okay?"

He was about to agree when he heard a sound that

triggered every internal red flag he had. Two pops, one then another, and he grabbed Rebecca and yanked her down to a crouch, then ran as fast as his gimp leg could take him until they'd reached the restraining wall that kept pedestrians from the City Hall building.

"What the—"

"Shh," he said, knowing he was freaking her out, but he had to get the message across fast and hard.

Rebecca froze as if he'd slapped her, which was good. He listened. For footsteps, for voices. There. To his left. Footsteps, heavy, moving slowly, coming right at them. He reached back and pulled Rebecca closer, put his coat across her face, then he tucked his head down, in case there were lights.

The footsteps got damn close, then continued on, still slow, still careful. Jake held steady until he could no longer hear them, then waited some more. Finally, he let her up.

"What the hell, Jake?" she whispered.

"Someone shot at us."

"What? I didn't hear anything."

"You didn't recognize the sound. It was suppressed. They used a silencer."

"Are you sure?"

He turned to face her. "I'd bet my life on it."

16

REBECCA HAD NO IDEA WHAT to make of any of this. She tried to remember the seconds before he'd pulled her down, but she couldn't recall any sounds at all. Jake seemed completely certain about the gunfire, but *gunfire?* Wasn't it more likely there were fireworks somewhere, or a car backfiring?

"Come on," he said, stepping over the barrier once again, holding her hand tight. "We have to get out of here now."

"Jake, wait. Just stop. I'm sure it sounded like a gunshot to you, but I swear, I didn't hear anything. We're in the middle of a park on a Wednesday night. Who would be shooting at us?"

He met her gaze, but only for a second. He was still scouring the shadows and the sidewalks, so focused she could feel the tremors in his hand. "You may be right, and I may be nuts, but I'm not willing to chance it, not with you here. We have to leave. Now. And we have to be quiet and quick."

She nodded. There was no point arguing. He kept them away from the lights, right against the barrier as they walked fast toward Broadway. Rebecca was the one who saw someone crouching by a fir tree. She yanked on Jake's hand, and when he glanced back, she pointed her chin.

He looked. "Shit," he said, then he was sprinting back from where they came, and this time, she heard it. A pop like a cork flying from a champagne bottle.

There was another pop, and this time, cement from the barricade in front of her splintered, making her gasp and cover her face as they ran. Jake pushed her over the barrier; his grunt when he landed next to her was a painful reminder of his limp and his pain.

"Keep down," he said. "I'll come get you in a second."

His hand disappeared and she panicked. "Jake." She remembered to whisper, but it didn't matter. He'd moved into an even deeper shadow between buildings. She covered her head with her arms, so afraid she could hardly breathe. Every second felt like her last, and she kept chanting his name over and over, trying to speed up time.

"Rebecca."

She jerked her head up. "Come on. Keep low."

Crouched over double, it was difficult as hell to walk, and it must have been ten times harder for Jake. He led her to the dark spot, and then he took her hand and brought it up against the wall.

The darkness was so complete she couldn't see spit, but she felt the edge of a doorway. Then nothing. A breeze. Startled, she jerked when he leaned in close to her head so he could whisper.

"I'm going to help you find the ladder that leads down from this doorway. You're not going to be able to see much when you start. In a minute though, you'll see blue. Those are the lights of the station below, and they'll stay on. They never go off. You'll adjust quickly to those lights, so don't be scared. I'll be right behind you, okay?"

She nodded. Then said, "Yes, okay."

It wasn't a simple thing, this maneuver. Because of the dark. Because she was shaking so badly. There was someone out there and he wasn't some random mugger. That gun had been aiming for her. For Jake. For both of them, either of them, it didn't matter. It was a real gun and real danger, and he was still out there.

The worst of it was the first step. It was as if nothing existed past the doorway. No staircase, no subway station, no earth at all. Nothing but a void, and all that was holding her from an endless fall was Jake, his hand steady, his voice so calm. "That's it. Easy does it. Just reach down with your right foot until you feel the step."

"I can't feel anything."

"Okay, okay. It's all right," he said, squeezing her hand. "Move your leg to the right. Swing it over nice and easy."

She obeyed him, but only because she was too petrified to do anything else. Then her foot hit against something metal. The thunk sounded thunderous.

"That's the ladder. That should help you get your bearings. Now you know where the side is, you can find the rung. Try again."

She did. She blinked trying to figure out if her eyes were open and maybe that was the scariest part. Not being able to tell. When her boot heel touched metal, she almost cried out, holding back the noise at the last second.

"Good, great. Firm your grip. The rest is simple, easy as can be. Really soon, there's going to be a blue light, and it'll come on gradually, but you'll see it, and you'll know you're halfway to the ground. Take your time, don't rush. You let me know when you're ready to let go, okay?"

She didn't think she'd ever be ready to let go of his hand, but this was no time to be a coward. He had to climb down, too. He must be terrified up there. And he knew what it felt like to get shot.

Oh, bad thought. She couldn't think about that now or she'd freeze. "Okay," she said and lowered herself until her left hand found the ladder. She'd never held on to anything so tightly.

"I'm right behind. I won't let anything happen to you. I swear."

"I know," she said, even though it felt as if her heart would beat straight out of her chest. But Jake had promised. He wasn't abandoning her; he was leading her to safety.

She stepped down with her other foot. Found the rung. Shifted her right hand. No turning back now, just down, just one step and another and the next and there. Blue. She didn't turn to find the source, just let the light filter into her field of vision. One step after another, and then she was seeing the wall, the ladder, her own hands. Miraculous. Weird. Real.

Looking up, she could make Jake out, too. Mostly his legs and his butt. By the time she got to the ground level, she felt more in control. She stepped away easily, even if she was more scared than she'd ever been in her life

Not thirty seconds later, Jake was beside her. "You okay?"

She nodded.

"Come on. I don't know how much they know about this station. But they're going to realize we came down at some point, so we'll head for the exit. I left the door open up there. If they try to get down the same way we did, it'll give us time to get out." He found her hand and turned.

"Wait," she said. "They?"

"Yeah. Two of them that I saw. I don't know if there are more."

She and Jake were speaking in whispers, but their voices echoed. In the distance, she heard a rumble. It was indistinct, more a feeling than a sound.

"But—"

"No time. We'll talk when we're safe. Stay close to me. The trains come through here. There are tracks, which means we have to be careful of the third rail, so no moving without me, got it? I can't use the flashlight. It's too dangerous. So stick close."

"Like glue," she said. She hadn't thought about the third rail. Despite not knowing what IRT stood for, she had taken the subway. She was a New Yorker, of course she had. So she'd known what the third rail was from the time she was a kid: Death. Big old nasty frying death.

So. Two gunmen. At least. Aiming for them. And now a third rail. Next time Jake asked her if she was ready for an adventure, she was going to say no. In the meantime, she slipped her free hand into his back pocket. That ought to keep her close enough.

JAKE IGNORED THE BURN IN his thigh and cursed himself for every kind of fool there'd ever been. He'd walked right into this. Shit. He'd been such an idiot.

T-Mac hadn't just taken the fall. He wasn't left there by accident. He'd made a deal with Keegan. He'd do the time for money. Had to be. That family in Georgia who called all the time? Jake had put out some feelers to find out about them, but hadn't gotten any return calls yet. He imagined they were living quite well.

Gary hadn't been able to dig up much of anything that wasn't on the official records about West, but he hadn't had a lot of free time to dedicate to the search. Why should he?

But Jake should have known better than to waltz into Sing Sing and announce his presence like a rank amateur. It hadn't even occurred to him that T-Mac and Keegan could have been in cahoots. Why not? Life with Packard and life in prison weren't that different except with prison there was a chance of parole. And when he got out, he'd be set. His family would be set. There was a money trail somewhere, and if Jake lived through this night, he was going to make it his business to find that trail and make sure both T-Mac and Keegan were tried for attempted murder.

First, though, he had to get Rebecca out of here in one piece. That's what made him the angriest. Not that he'd been an idiot—he'd been a dope plenty of times before. Never when it cost so much, and never, never when he had something so precious in his care.

He should have kept his suspicions to himself. He should have kept his mouth shut and done his digging on his own time.

The train that had been way the hell down the line was now coming on fast. There were still work lights up, so he could get them safely behind the concrete wall that kept the maintenance crews from accidentally getting run over.

He released her hand and covered her ears with his palms; the trains made an ungodly screech as they took the curve of this loop of track. The squeal of metal against metal echoed back on itself, bouncing off the tile walls of the station. Under that was the noise of the train itself, which sounded like an earthquake this close. He surrounded Rebecca as much as he could with his body and his hands as the train rumbled and screamed, and he felt her press in, gripping his back for all she was worth.

Jesus, she had to be okay. Whoever these guys were, they weren't sharpshooters, but he'd wager a great deal that they weren't willing to turn up empty-handed at the end of the night. West's whole world was being threatened, and he wasn't going to hire muscle on the cheap.

Jake would have to be smarter, that's all. Whoever they were, they didn't know this station. He did. Every nook and cranny, and that was what would save them. He already knew there was no cell phone reception in the station. But there were call boxes, if he could get to one.

He winced as the sound assaulted his ears, knowing it would take some time before they'd be able to hear each other. The worst of it passed and he slowly stepped back from Rebecca, checking to make sure she was all right.

She gave him a smile. Not a big one, but a brave one, and he kissed her, then guided her hand to his back pocket and they were on the move.

They got across the tracks fine, and then they followed the curve of the platform, hugging the walls. Halfway to the exit stairs, he saw one of the gunmen on the right edge of the stairs coming down, his gun held in both hands, his head moving so he could sweep the area. No flashlight, but then he didn't need one yet.

Quietly and smoothly, Jake moved backward about fifteen feet, guiding Rebecca. He felt his way to the alcove, a niche built into the wall that had been his favorite place to hide while showing his friends around, the better to scare the crap out of them when he jumped out. He'd been such an ass.

It was a tight fit for two, but that was okay. He turned her sideways, then pushed in himself. Face-to-face. He could look out beyond her to see where the gunmen were. If they weren't both down here, they would be soon. Now, Jake would listen. Wait. After a quick check to make sure he was in the clear, he bent and got a couple of good stones for throwing. Maybe he could get one of them to step on the tracks. Maybe he could get them close enough and push one of them himself.

In the meantime, he had to protect her as best he could. She was trembling like a leaf. He wasn't much better. No weapon, no way of reaching help. Her life depending on his wits and his speed. Standing here without much range of motion was about the worst thing he could do as far as his leg went.

He leaned in close to Rebecca's ear until his lips brushed the silky lobe. "We wait now," he whispered as softly as he could. "We have home turf advantage. We're going to be fine. I'm sorry I can't show you where you are. It's so beautiful, sweetheart. Colored glass, tiles of green, tan and white up to the ceiling in the four corners of the vault over the mezzanine. The skylights are amazing. Imagine great pools of natural light from up above, and when they're not enough, they brought in brass chandeliers," he said, trying to distract her but she was still shaking. "The architect who designed the arches was famous back then. A showman. His name was Rafael Guastavino."

Jake looked out again, hating the vulnerability of sticking his neck out, but he did it, and it was a damn good thing, because both men were down the stairs, and one of them was walking toward their alcove.

Jake ducked back, then pressed them both, hard, against the back of the cubbyhole. It was dark, very dark, and as long as the man didn't flash a light directly at them, he'd never know the alcove existed, let alone that they were hiding in it.

His footsteps seemed as loud as the train had been at its worst. Slow, taking his time. But then a real rumble started behind him. Another train. The man needed to hurry. Step up his pace. Get past them, well past them to the walkway leading down to the dark end of the tunnel.

He needed the man to be far enough that when the train came, he and Rebecca could make a break for the stairs. It would be so loud the gunmen would never hear them. Jake knew exactly where to go, where to hide, but he needed a few minutes' grace. It didn't seem like too much to ask for, so he did, until the sound of the train ground in his chest. He took hold of Rebecca's hand, squeezed it tight. Prayed he could move fast enough.

When the conductor's car was twenty feet away, Jake broke out, pulling her behind him. Not too fast, even though he wanted to sprint. Not until she caught up to him, and then they hauled ass. Fuck the leg, screw the pain, they were running up the stairs, the screech of the train filling the platform to the rafters. They were soundless, they were panting and then they were past the curve and up the second shorter set of stairs and he could see where those bastards had broken in. No locks to mess with meant he could get her out more quickly. Good. The final steps, leading up to the sidewalk, and she surged in front of him, pulling him with her, and thank God for that because his leg was about ready to quit.

He yanked his phone out of his pocket, but she

wouldn't stop. Not until they got to the street and she'd waved down a cab and shoved him inside.

While he called the 1st Precinct, she gave the cabbie an address. Jake told the desk who he was, including his old badge number, that there were armed men in the City Hall Station and that they'd be gone damn soon, so get there fast.

He hung up after giving his callback number, pulled her into a fierce kiss, squeezing her too tightly, and, shit, he couldn't breathe, but he didn't care. But *she* needed to breathe so he backed off and met her gaze. "You okay?"

"Scared out of my mind. I can hardly believe what just happened. It's insane."

"But you're okay. You're not hurt."

"Yes. Yes, I'm fine. We're going to Charlie's and we'll figure it all out there."

"Good," he said, then he bent over and pressed down on his thigh as he tried like hell not to scream. Her hand was on his back and she was talking.

"It's okay, honey. You were fantastic. You're going to be fine. You got us out. We're safe now. It's okay. Please, be okay."

JAKE DIDN'T RECOGNIZE THE building they were dropped at, but it didn't surprise him that it was where her cousin Charlie lived, considering it was directly across the street from the park on Central Park West.

Getting out of the cab and into the elevator was something he could have lived his whole life without, but Rebecca was a champ. She did all of the heavy lifting. He tried not to make any sounds, but then he'd step down and a muscle would spasm and it was like being shot all over again.

The elevator opened to Charlie and Bree looking worried. And confused.

"What's going on? You were pretty damn cryptic," Charlie said, but Bree shoved him to the side so she could put Jake's other arm around her shoulder and help him into the house. Apartment. Palace.

"Maybe we should call an ambulance," Bree said, trying to help him to the couch, but not succeeding very well.

"No. I don't need an ambulance. I need to take my pain medication. It's muscle and nerve damage from doing too much. It'll settle down."

Charlie left. Rebecca and Bree hovered. It was sweet, but what he needed was a few minutes alone. He was about to do some major cussing and there might even be some crying involved, and he'd prefer not to have any witnesses for that. Especially not Rebecca.

He got his pill bottle out of his pocket and winced at how his hand shook as he opened it. He wanted to take two, but that would make him groggy, and he couldn't afford that now. One wasn't going to kick this. Not without some serious muscle work, but it would help. Charlie came back with a glass. Jake didn't spill much, only on his jeans. Someone took the glass and he breathed as deeply as he could, trying to remember what Taye said about letting the pain in, not fighting it.

There were too many people, too many thoughts. He couldn't stop and he wasn't going to hold it together much longer.

Rebecca took a couple of steps back. "I need a drink," she said. "You two, come with me, and I'll catch you up."

"I'll be right there," Charlie said.

There might have been a struggle, but it was silent and Jake gave up trying to figure it out. When he opened his eyes again, Charlie was still there. "Do I need to call an attorney? My man on retainer is excellent."

Jake shook his head. "You need to get Rebecca somewhere safe. William West is an ex-drug trafficker I ran into a dozen years ago. It's too long a story to go into. But I recognized him. He sent a couple of guys to kill me. Rebecca was collateral damage." He looked up at Charlie. "I put her life in danger. I almost got her killed. You have to get her away, understand? Out of town. Out of the state."

Jake forced himself to his feet even though the pain threatened to shut him down for good. But he took hold of Charlie's shirt and looked him square in the eyes. "Goddammit, *I almost got her killed.*" Charlie nodded. His face narrowed to a pinprick of light, then nothing.

17

Rebecca was sitting next to him on the couch. She looked pale and shaken as she held his hand. Shit. He must have blacked out for a minute. "What are you still doing here? You have to go."

She gently pushed him back down when he tried to get up. "It's okay. Calm down. Your pill hasn't kicked in yet."

"You don't get it. Keegan didn't just steal the money from Packard, he made a deal with T-Mac. The guy in Sing Sing. He paid T-Mac to take the fall. They've been working together all this time. I went in and spilled everything to T-Mac. He called West, and that's why those men were trying to kill us. Kill me. I'm sorry. I never should have said anything to you. I know, it's all my fault, but it doesn't matter now because Keegan knows you're with me so you're in danger. You have to leave. Now."

"Sweetie, it wasn't your fault," she said. "It wasn't you. It was me. The way I was staring at West over dinner. He knew I was looking for scars."

Jake sat up straighter and turned his hand so he was holding hers. He didn't think he'd been out long. Charlie was where he'd left him, but Bree was in his arms now. Fine. Good, but no one seemed to be getting the big picture. The danger wasn't over.

He turned back to Rebecca, mulling over what she'd said. "No way he would have made that connection," he murmured, knowing she wasn't necessarily wrong. Of course it wasn't her fault, but Keegan had to be paranoid returning to New York and anything could've set him off.

She shook her head. "But he did. I thought it was something else, I thought he was trying to figure out how to get in my pants. The way he stared at me. He knew something was wrong. I thought I was being subtle, but I wasn't. I was practically painting him a picture."

"It sounds like it was a combination of both those things," Charlie said, echoing Jake's thoughts. "The guy's been on the run for, what, twelve years? Anything could have tipped him off. Blame isn't the point. What do we do next?"

"We can't do anything until Jake can think without pain," Rebecca said. "Isn't there anything we can do for you?"

Jake shook his head, tried again to get up. How Keegan had put two and two together wasn't important now. Rebecca's safety was. "The only thing that will help me is for you to get the hell out of here. I mean it, Rebecca." He looked at Charlie. "What the fuck is wrong with you? I told you to get her out of the city."

Rebecca grabbed his chin and turned his head so he was facing her. "They're after you, too, goddammit, and I'm not leaving without you."

He'd never heard her swear like that and it stopped him. He glanced at Charlie, who had a faint smile tugging at his mouth. What the hell was wrong with these rich people? Did they think they were immune from danger? "Those were real guns, with real ammo. They meant you to die. They aren't finished. Your home isn't safe. You're not safe. Do me a favor and go. Hire a car. Don't go back to your place. Just get to the airport. Not LaGuardia, go to Newark. Go anywhere. Pay cash. And do it now please. I'm begging you. I have things to do, and I can't even think straight while you're still here."

"Ah," she said, nodding. "I get it now."

"Thank God," he said, putting his hand on his leg, feeling instantly that it was way too soon to even try to work on the muscle.

"But," Rebecca said, "I'm not leaving without you."

Jake stilled. What was it going to take? He ignored her and looked to Charlie and Bree. "A little help would be good here, people. I know you care about her. I can't imagine any of you want to go to her funeral."

"Rebecca," Charlie said, releasing Bree from his hold. "You're with me. Bree? Find out what this madman needs, and let's get this show on the road. I don't want to go to anyone's funeral."

Rebecca glared at him, then Charlie gave her a look that spoke of years of collusion. She wasn't happy about it, but she got up from the couch, squeezing Jake's hand before she walked away with Charlie.

Jake leaned back on the couch. Now that he had an ally, he could think clearly. At least that was his goal.

"What can I do?" Bree asked.

"I need to find out if the police got to those shooters. And how we can connect the shooters to either T-Mac or West, preferably both. I need to call Crystal Farrington. She's an assistant D.A. who knows all about this." He dug into his pocket for his wallet, the small movement making him wince. But there was her phone number. He'd call as soon as the spasm that was clawing through his quad let him go.

REBECCA TURNED ON HER cousin the minute the kitchen door swung shut. "I'm not leaving without him, Charlie. I don't know what you expect to accomplish, but changing my mind is not going to happen."

"Yeah, I got that," he said, smiling so smugly she wanted to slap him.

"Then what's with the 'Rebecca, you're with me' bullcrap?"

"Your cop needs to get his act together, and you being in his face wasn't helpful. The danger here is real, so we'd better figure out a way to get his goals accomplished while you're still in the house. Frankly, I don't like the idea that killers could be after you. You're the only relative I like. You're not checking out until we're old and decrepit."

"Oh. I thought you were going to argue with me."

"Nope. Before your little declaration there, I was going to tell you to fight for Jake. That he's the keeper you're always harping about. But you obviously have that covered, so now we can move on to practical matters. Like staying out of his way. At least for a while."

She hugged Charlie, real quick because they weren't the hugging type, and then she settled. "The way I see it, he only has a limited amount of focus at the moment. I'll keep back. Not away, because if something happens I need to be close, but I won't be obvious. I'll listen. So you'll have to be his sounding board. He'll know what to do, Charlie. He may not have his badge, but he's a damn good cop."

"Fine. You hang, I'll distract, and we'll get you both safe."

"THANKS, CRYSTAL. KEEP ME in the loop, and I'll do the same." Jake hung up the phone and looked at Charlie, who'd suddenly appeared in front of the couch.

"Who was in charge of the original operation?" Charlie asked.

"Wait your turn," Bree said before she addressed Jake. "I have a wet/dry heating pad. I'm thinking moist heat. Would that help?"

Jake looked at her, and he couldn't help smiling. She was wearing an obnoxiously bright orange sweater over a green skirt. "Yeah. Thanks. That would help." She hustled off, and he faced Charlie again. "She's not gone. I would know if she was gone."

"She's making the arrangements. Right now. So, tell me what you need to get West behind bars."

Jake had brought Crystal up to speed, and she was going to work on getting T-Mac's phone records, this time through legit channels because this time, they would need it in court. Dammit, how long did it take to get a car here to Central Park West? It wasn't like Brook— "Shit, I have to call my old man."

Blessedly, Charlie and Bree left him alone while he dialed his father. Jake had already asked the department to send a couple of uniforms to watch the house, but he wouldn't tell his father. That would just piss him off. He switched on the speaker since he thought he could work on his leg now. Besides, his dad knew about the Keegan/West connection, so there wasn't much to say, except that Jake might have put him in danger. Him and Pete and Liam.

"Don't you worry about us, Jakey," his father said, and it was like they were on the walkie-talkies. "We have about a hundred years of experience between us. And a goddamn arsenal. I hope those bastards do come here. We'll teach 'em what NYPD cops are made of."

"Don't take any chances, Dad." Jake used both thumbs on the peripheral muscles, working his way inward. "Please. Just, see if you can go stay with Liam, huh? Get out of there, at least until we know what to do."

"I'll tell you exactly what I'm going to do, son. I'm going to call Dan Reaves is what. He'll get a judge to sign the warrants to get into West's business, and the prison phone records, and damn near anything else he can once I tell him what's what. He's tried to live that bust down all his career. He wants Keegan. More than you do."

"He tried to kill Rebecca, old man. No one wants Keegan more than I do."

His father was quiet for a long moment, long enough for Jake to remember how she'd trembled in his arms, how brave she'd been. How he'd move heaven and earth for her if he could, but he was useless like this.

"You're right, Jake. Your job now is to keep her safe. I'll call Dan—we go way back. I'll keep you informed. He'll probably want to talk to you so make sure you have that phone on. And take a goddamn pill, I can hear the pain in your voice."

"Tell Reaves to get in touch with Crystal Farrington at the D.A.'s office. She's working on the phone records from Sing Sing, but she could use some backup."

"Farrington. Got it."

"Thanks, Dad," Jake said.

"No sweat."

"Hey, Pop, how many cops does it take to screw in a lightbulb?"

"How many?"

Jake smiled. "None. It turned itself in."

His father laughed as Jake hung up. Then he felt Rebecca's hand on his shoulder as she leaned over the couch and kissed him like she'd never let him go.

It took two hours, but Rebecca and Jake finally made it into the Town Car that Charlie had hired. Jake had walked without assistance, but his limp was awful and he still looked too pale. She'd packed some food for the ride. Nothing much, just some protein bars and juice; they'd grab something better at the airport.

She pressed herself against him, hardly believing everything that had happened in such a short period of time. The shooting, the trip down the ladder, the terrifying sound of echoing footsteps all felt more like something she'd read than something that she'd lived through.

But he'd brought her out safely. This amazing man. Listening as he'd talked to the two policeman who'd come to Charlie's had been an education in itself. Of course she'd known Jake was a cop; he'd demonstrated that in his every action tonight, in his instincts that had ferreted out a killer. But she'd been utterly captivated and impressed with his logic, his approach to finding the critical proof that would connect T-Mac to West.

"You're an incredible policeman," she said. "Not only were you right about everything—"

He opened his mouth in what she knew would be a protest, but she stopped him with two fingers on his lips.

"—but you saved my life."

"Your life shouldn't have been in danger in the first place," he said.

"Hmm. The correct response should have been 'You're welcome, Rebecca.'"

Jake ran his knuckles down her jaw. "The thought of losing you…"

"We're both here, and we're relatively fine. We'll be better once we're wherever we're going. Any thoughts on that?"

"I have no idea," he said. "Vegas is out."

She grinned. "No passports, so we can't leave the country. But those can be sent to us so our first destination doesn't have to be our last. We had talked about Paris."

"We probably won't be gone that long. Phone calls were made tonight, or an email, or whatever, which gives us a window of time to focus the search on how West and T-Mac connected. How West contacted the shooter. T-Mac is in Sing Sing. Somewhere, there's a record. As soon as they can latch on to anything concrete, then they'll go after Keegan with both barrels. That'll be our cue to come back. We could have that connection by morning."

"We wouldn't have to come back right away, would we?"

He smiled. "What did you have in mind?"

"Time. Alone with you. You know, to begin."

"Begin?"

She shifted in her seat until she was facing him. "You do realize that when I said I wasn't leaving without you, I meant forever."

Jake's smile vanished and his jaw slackened as he leaned toward her. "Rebecca."

"Oh, God. You don't want— I'm sorry, I thought—"

"No, no." He took both her hands and squeezed them. "I do. I…I didn't know you wanted—"

"I did. I do."

"How?" he asked, and it was so earnest and hopeful she teared up again.

"I couldn't see it before either," she said. "Even though I'd fallen totally in love with you, I couldn't see how we could make it work. And then tonight, I got it. All the things I was worried about were just logistics. Everything important is you. That we're together."

"But I don't have a job, I've got my Dad—"

"You've got disability, so that's fine. Look, if you'd cared about the money, this never would have happened. So we make it work. Oh."

"What?"

"We can't be gone for too long. Imagine what the boys are going to do to your place? It'll look like an armored frat house."

Jake smiled. "Yeah, pizza boxes to the ceiling." He touched her hair. "What about the foundation?"

"It's not going to fall apart. And we'll get your father's new bathroom in shape when we get back. Then we'll figure it out. Day by day. If you want to."

"*We'll* get Dad's bathroom in shape?"

"Yes, we."

"You trying to get into my tool belt?"

She traced his endearing crooked smile with the tip of her unsteady finger. To not have this face…this man in her life…was unthinkable. The thought terrified her more than the threat of West on their heels. "Always, and I'm quite good at getting my way."

He kissed her then, deeply. She kissed him back with every promise she could make. When she pulled back, it was only to tell him, "I'll never feel safer than in your arms."

"I'll never let anyone harm you," he whispered back. "You're all that matters. You're all that will ever matter to me."

* * * * *

Sizzling fairy tales to make every fantasy come true!

Fan-favorite authors

Tori Carrington and Kate Hoffmann

bring readers

Blazing Bedtime Stories, Volume VI

MAID FOR HIM...

Successful businessman Kieran Morrison doesn't dare hope for a big catch when he goes fishing. But when he wakes up one night to find a beautiful woman seemingly unconscious on the deck of his sailboat, he lands one bigger than he could ever have imagined by way of mermaid Daphne Moore. But is she real? Or just a fantasy?

OFF THE BEATEN PATH

Greta Adler and Alex Hansen have been friends for seven years. So when Greta agrees to accompany Alex at a mountain retreat owned by a client, she doesn't realize that Alex has a different path he wants their relationshiop to take. But will Greta follow his lead?

Available April 2012 wherever books are sold.

www.Harlequin.com

HB79679

Taft Bowman knew he'd ruined any chance he'd had for happiness with Laura Pendleton when he drove her away years ago...and into the arms of another man, thousands of miles away. Now she was back, a widow with two small children...and despite himself, he was starting to believe in second chances.

A younger woman stood there, and from this distance he had only a strange impression, as though she was somehow standing on an island of calm amid the chaos of the scene, the flashing lights of the emergency vehicles, shouts between his crew members, the excited buzz of the crowd.

And then the woman turned and he just about tripped over a snaking fire hose somebody shouldn't have left there.

Laura.

He froze, and for the first time in fifteen years as a firefighter, he forgot about the incident, his mission, just what the hell he was doing here.

Laura.

Ten years. He hadn't seen her in all that time, since the week before their wedding when she had given him back his ring and left town. Not just town. She had left the whole damn country, as if she couldn't run far enough to get away from him.

Some part of him desperately wanted to think he had made some kind of mistake. It couldn't be her. That was just some other slender woman with a long sweep of honey-blond hair and big, blue, unforgettable eyes. But no. It was definitely Laura. Sweet and lovely.

Not his.

He was going to have to go over there and talk to her. He didn't want to. He wanted to stand there and pretend he hadn't seen her. But he was the fire chief. He couldn't hide out just because he had a painful history with the daughter of the property owner.

Sometimes he hated his job.

Will Taft and Laura be able to make the years recede...or is the gulf between them too broad to ever cross?

Find out in
A COLD CREEK REUNION
Available April 2012 from Harlequin® Special Edition®
wherever books are sold.

HSEEXP0412